Hope Sheffield

The Inflatable Man

This is a work of fiction. Names and characters are the product of the author's imagination and any resemblance to actual persons, living or dead, is entirely coincidental.

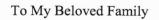

To My Beloved Family

Chapter One

Thursday, April 4, 1996

"Pardon me, Ma'am. Mind if I join you?"

The stranger laid his hand on the back of the chair beside Suzanna. He did it casually, as if he had a right to touch this extension of her. The hand was broad and calloused with neatly trimmed nails, the dark hairs on its back multiplying as they swarmed up his naked arm to the coarse, ingratiating face, his gray-brown hair slicked back after some effort with a cheap comb and a tube of Vaseline. He wore a short-sleeved plaid sport shirt, unbuttoned at the throat to reveal those same dark hairs, a mass of them now, like an animal held in check. Then the hand gripped and pulled, the bicep tensing as he slid the chair out from the table, the chair that felt attached to her like a limb. She could feel that hand touching her, the rough Indiana farm skin rubbing against her creamed Kenilworth matron skin, at the same time that she could see it next to her, still holding the chair. Suzanna pushed herself back and stood, tripping away.

"I'm sorry, I'm afraid I'm finished," she said.

She snatched her purse and fled from her untouched meal, through the restaurant smell of roast beef and Thousand Island dressing and chlorine from the pool, through the lobby to the elevator. She heard his feet relentless behind her, and she felt his hand on her back, the grain of his skin rough even through her linen jacket. Turning quickly, sure she would feel his breath, that she would have to shove him and perhaps even scream, she saw that he wasn't there.

The bell rang, the elevator doors opened, and Suzanna stepped in, followed closely by two men in suits.

"Nasty weather. Damp," one of them mentioned.

They were business travelers like herself, but crucially different, and they gestured for her to press her floor button first, in acknowledgement of her breasts and her vulnerability. She pushed number five, which lit from the heat of her hand. A fat index finger reached across her to touch seven. Now she wondered if she had been tricked, if the men had exchanged silent, comprehending looks, planning to take advantage of this chance alone with her, to step out behind her into the empty fifth floor corridor and slam her up against the ice machine, her beige skirt quickly bunched around her waist, her stockings in tatters.

"I never saw so much snow as last February. Glad to have that over," said the other man.

"Yup. Spring is better, even if it is wet."

The number five above illuminated, the doors slid open, and the men stepped aside to let her pass. Suzanna hurried down the hallway to her room, tugged the magnetic card from her purse, jammed it into the lock, opened the door, rushed in, and bolted it behind her.

Suzanna set her purse on the desk beside her briefcase, a gift from Power Health Corporation six months ago when she began her training as sales representative for the northern Midwest region. Her friends had thought she was completely deranged. After all, her husband Bob was a senior vice president at First Chicago, they owned their gracious Kenilworth Colonial, and they had long since saved the money for Chris's Princeton education. For years Suzanna's life had been the twice-weekly ladies lunch, tennis and the odd P.T.A. meeting, sweater shopping and matching pillow shams, filling the empty hours until Chris came home from school, a focal point which shifted bewilderingly towards evening as he grew older. But now Chris was in college, and Bob didn't get home until eight or even nine these days, and she couldn't fill that much time. And she worried over the picture of her life, precious moments frittered away on ephemeral amusements except for raising Chris. And Catie. She had raised Catie for a while, and that mattered too, despite its brevity.

Bob had been surprisingly supportive of her decision to take the Power Health job. She had always considered him a traditional, dinner-on-the-table-when-I-come-home-from-a-hard-day's-work sort of man, but perhaps he had evolved with their change of situation. Suzanna liked the idea of travel, of getting out in the world, away from her pristine house and her manicured friends and her eight block route from the house to the post office to the grocery store. But she hadn't realized how vulnerable she would feel alone among strangers, specifically, strange men. It was silly, she was safe in her room now, bolted against even a passkey -- could a passkey turn the privacy lock? And she wondered if her intense awareness of men, of the possibility of sex and violence, might reveal some dark, secret wish which could only express itself as fear.

Maybe some talk, a normal chat with normal Bob, would ground her again. Stepping out of her high heels, Suzanna picked up the telephone and punched in the interminable sequence of credit card and home numbers. Not that their relationship was particularly close, but warmth and Bob simply did not go together anymore. Suzanna had learned to accept his distance, to recognize the dominant social pattern, the romantic wife and the weary husband, the eternal mismatch.

She would tell him about the man in the restaurant. Tucked safely in her room now, she could make a joke out of it, or flaunt it a little, to make him jealous. Could she still make Bob jealous? A dashing -- well, perhaps in some barnyard circles, she wouldn't mention that -- older man had tried to sit down with her, and he was quite persistent, but she had, of course, rejected him. The attention shouldn't surprise Bob. Suzanna had always been cute, and she had made a successful transition to middle age, with her blonde highlights and her career-woman wardrobe. Her usual careful application of pink lipstick, golden brown eyeliner, and blush painted her pale features into a delicate prettiness. Still, husbands could be astonishingly blind.

The phone rang twice. Bob was probably dozing in front of "Wall Street Week" with a Heineken. He would have to rouse himself, rest his bottle on a botanic print coaster, or, more likely, a newspaper section, hoist himself from the wing chair, and cross the family room to the kitchen desk. Suzanna let the phone ring four times and then hung up quickly, before the answering machine could click on. She checked her diamond watch, which Bob had given her eleven years ago, after

8

Catie was born. It was eight-fifteen. He had certainly been working hard these past few months -- odd, given his seniority, but she brushed the vague doubt from her mind. She punched in his office number, which rang until voice mail picked up.

"Hello, this is Robert Healey. Please leave a message after the tone."

Maybe he wouldn't have been such a comfort after all, Suzanna thought. His voice had the cold rasp that she had first noticed after Catie died, from holding back his grief. But it hadn't changed in all these years, since April 6, 1990, six years ago this Saturday. She shivered.

"Bob, it's me. I'm at some God-forsaken Holiday Inn in Indiana. I left you the number by the kitchen phone, I can't tell what it is from the label here. Please call me when you get home. Please -- I --."

Her throat caught, and she hung up. She wished she hadn't lost control, sounding so desperate at the end. She wanted to be sophisticated, like the women he worked with, like that Treena person she had met at the bank Christmas party last year, not some pitiful housewife in over her head. That was the problem with answering machine messages. The beep always caught you by surprise, and you said something stupid, and then it was too late, you couldn't change it.

Suzanna padded over to the door and checked the locks. Yes, she had bolted them. She had even flipped the latch, though she doubted it even was a latch, probably a doorstop. She went into the immaculate bathroom, unwrapped a miniature bar of soap, and washed her face. The floor was cold, and everything was sterile, wrapped rolls of stiff toilet paper lined up along the mirror. She went back into the bedroom, sat on one of the two double beds, and stared at the phone. She could try calling Chris at Princeton, but the chances of his being in his room were slim, and she didn't want to disturb him with her foolish worries. She was the mother, after all.

As she stared, willing Bob to call her, the red light began to flicker, and the phone began to ring.

"Hello?" she asked, her voice cautious.

"Suzanna? It's Frank. Are you okay?"

Oh, Frank, how nice of you to call."

"I just wanted to see how you were doing down there, make sure everything was going all right, whatever."

Frank tried to sound gruff, but she could tell that her eager reception pleased him. He was her boss, the owner of Power Health, and a sweet, lonely man. He had told her about his recent divorce over lunch one day, surprisingly, since he was ordinarily a stickler for decorum. He wouldn't go on an overnight business trip with her, for example. That was silly, of course, he was a balding, fiftyish man with a paunch, and she already had one of those at home. Besides, she didn't want to be a snob, but their social backgrounds were so different, no one could possibly imagine anything beyond a business friendship between them.

"Everything is fine. The meeting with the employee benefits people went well, and I'll be seeing Mr. Porter first thing in the morning."

"That's great, I knew you could do it. Though I don't want you to get too comfortable without me -- I'll still be coming with you to Detroit next week." He laughed awkwardly. "So, did you find a decent dinner down there -- probably chicken fried steak, home fries, and a tossed salad with tomato wedges and blue cheese dressing, am I right?"

"Well, I'm afraid I didn't get to enjoy the local cuisine. I was in the dining room downstairs, my meal had just arrived, and a man came over and started to bother me."

"My God, that's terrible -- what did he do -- are you all right?"

"Oh yes, I'm fine, just a little hungry. He wanted to sit with me, he was really quite persistent, he wouldn't take no for an answer. And he was coming up quite close to me, and he touched me once, I think. It just upset me, that's all." It had all come out in a rush.

"Imagine, preying on an innocent woman alone, a fine woman like you. My God, that makes me sick. I'll tell you what I'm going to do, I'm going to get in my car right now and come down there. This is my fault, I shouldn't have sent you alone. It won't take me long. Just keep your door locked. I'm leaving now, and I should be there by -- two A.M."

Suzanna laughed. "Honestly, Frank, that's not necessary. I'm fine. My door is locked, and he didn't follow me, and I'll be leaving in the morning. I'm sure I won't see him again."

"Only if you're completely certain -- ."

"Yes, I'm certain."

"I just don't want anything to happen to you, Suzanna."

"Thanks. To tell you the truth, I was a little shaken up, but you've made me feel a lot better. It's nice to know someone cares."

"Well, I do. Sure you don't want me to come?"

11

"Yes, but thanks. I'll talk to you tomorrow. Goodnight."

"Goodnight."

Suzanna could feel Frank lingering on the line as she firmly hung up. Despite her control on the telephone, she felt a bit flustered. Frank had expressed a concern for her far beyond anything she would expect even from Bob. He seemed passionately interested in her. And although she didn't want to admit it, she felt the stirrings of a response -- a combination of amusement, attraction, and fear.

At fifty, Bob Healey was a silver banker bird, his beak protruding beneath blinking blue eyes and a crest of receding gray hair. At eight o'clock Thursday night, he swooped through the darkened passageways of his aerie, past empty chairs and silent computers, into Treena Snider's office. Treena had gone home to her daughters and her husband Craig, as she did every night of her dogged existence, this purgatory before the beginning of her heavenly life with Bob.

He flipped a switch, and the fluorescent light crackled, illuminating her neat desk, the chair which had cradled her, and framed prints of impressionist flower gardens. He smiled at her naiveté, the innocent female spirit glowing even in this utilitarian cubicle. Treena was created for love, not to shuffle papers in a cage under harsh light. She was only working to put bread in the mouths of the beautiful children that her husband Craig was too dim-witted to support.

12

Bob circled the desk and sank into Treena's chair. It still felt warm to him, impossibly -- she had left, as she always did, three hours ago, promptly at five o'clock. His fingers brushed the photograph propped in a ceramic frame on the corner of her desk. Ellie and Jane, Treena's daughters, smiled sunnily, blonde hair curling from under straw hats, chubby arms folded over matching pink dresses. They looked so alike, they could be the same child at different ages. The older of the two, Ellie, was five, just the age Catie had been, and with the same pale radiance. Bob imagined Ellie, how soft she would feel when he hugged her. And he thought about Treena, so full of life and possibilities.

His elbows behind his head, Bob settled back. Certainly, he and Suzanna had had a decent run. They had bought a house and participated in community affairs and raised a family of sorts, but that was past. All they could do now was deteriorate together, a fate not even Suzanna, with her new job and interests, appeared willing to accept. Bob supposed she would balk when he told her he was marrying Treena, but she couldn't expect him to sacrifice his entire life for her. Marrying Treena was solid constructive thinking, the kind of forward-looking vision that had made him a senior vice-president. He wasn't going to waste time feeling guilty about it.

He leaned forward again to admire the girls. As he stared, their edges blurred, until they seemed to be one person, his own daughter. He lifted the frame, then turned it over and unhooked its cardboard backing. As he had anticipated, Treena had saved earlier pictures behind the current one. Bob took the most recent one, then fastened the frame and repositioned it on Treena's desk.

The photograph tucked safely in his breast pocket, Bob returned to his own office. There, he removed it and kissed the girls tenderly, his lips covering their whole faces. Placing them carefully inside his top desk drawer, he noticed the flashing phone message light. He punched in the computer number of his voice mail system.

"Bob, it's me. I'm at some God-forsaken Holiday Inn . . ."

He had forgotten that Suzanna was away tonight. She sounded stressed, but she was forty-five years old, it was time she learned to stand on her own two feet. She would be forced to soon enough.

"Hey, you're drinking the whole thing! Gimme that!"

Chris Healey grabbed Phillip's beer mid-chug, splashing it down the front of Phillip's favorite "Party On" tee shirt. Listing, Chris wiped his mouth with his forearm and belched.

"You're an animal, know that, Chris?"

"Yuh. Thanks."

It was Thursday night at Princeton, but in Chris's freshman suite the weekend had already begun. Chris and his roommates, Phillip and Derek, shared three rooms and a bath at the top of a gray stone turret in a crumbling dorm near the center of the campus.

"Hey, you're slopping all over the oriental," Chris protested, as Phillip held the mug upside down over his

14

face. Chris hated squishing across the rug to the chilly bathroom in the middle of the night.

"That's no oriental, it's from T.J. Maxx. Lo, when I sit enshrined in this ivory tower, my mind oft succumbs to the ghosts of luminaries who haunt the corridors of this auspicious institution. Just think -- F. Scott Fitzgerald might have flunked out in this very room. It's inspiring." Phillip plopped onto the ripped couch and rested his feet on the coffee table, an enormous wooden spool that had once wound some gigantic cable-like substance, to ponder life's grand coincidences. He was tall and wiry, with dark hair and the vestiges of acne, in contrast to Chris's fair-haired boy, blue eyes and baby skin, his father's hawk nose softened with a dash of Suzanna's daintiness.

At first, Chris had thought this set-up awesome, the turret was, like, gothic, and they had a lot of space. But by the end of the first week, his enthusiasm had waned. Although willing to pump iron in a proper health club, he objected to climbing four flights of stairs just to get his books, and hauling up a simple keg of beer was a nightmare. Also, it didn't take differential calculus to determine that, if the three of them wanted to maintain one of their three rooms as a living room for parties, which they absolutely did, that meant two people had to share a bedroom each semester, and one person had to do it all year. To his dismay, Chris discovered that, in this important real-world situation, his stellar high school credentials and boyish good looks didn't mean squat. He had drawn the paper with the X, and he could neither charm nor bribe his way out of it. Chris was not so shallow, however, as to permit these petty indignities to completely disenchant him. He still admired the leaded glass in the bedroom he now shared with Derek, and when he was drunk, which was generally from Thursday through Sunday, he stared out through its rippley diamonds at the blurred, gray quad and felt honestly moved to be a Princeton man.

"You're just pissed because you don't get to go to Mexico on Saturday," Phillip noted, "but don't take it out on me. I'm sorry for you, Buddy -- I mean, what's spring break without a few nachos and muchachas, and a little fun in the old el sol? But hey, I guess you'll finally get that bedroom to yourself."

Chris shrugged and flopped onto a lounge chair, its gray stuffing adhering to his pants. "Who can explain parents? I mean, here I am, their hot shot son, straight A's at New Trier, track team, swim meets, school musicals -- I can just hear my father in this low voice he uses when he confides in random strangers, 'Of course, my son is at Princeton. You know, I went to Princeton too. Well, the apple doesn't fall far from the tree -- a law of Newtonian physics, I believe.' Well, if he's so god damned proud of me, which I richly deserve, I am any North Shore parent's god damned dream son, why don't I get to go to Mexico with my friends for one lousy week like everybody else?"

"I don't know, Chris, I can't explain it. Parents can be truly imponderable." Phillip shook his head sagely. "It is a huge disappointment."

"Yeah, well it is. They seem to think they're doing it for my own good, some bullshit about my grades being down and a nice, quiet week to catch up on 'my studies' -- don't they know about the dangers of adolescent depression? It's freezing cold, there aren't any leaves on the trees, I haven't seen an actual color in

16

months. People commit suicide from that kind of stress. You'd think they'd rather have me re-energizing for a serious end-of-the-semester push than splattering myself all over the sidewalk. What would they have to brag about then? Their promising son who departed life too soon, with so many prizes left to win and so much money to make. But ah, the memories." Chris stopped. The faint image of a five-year-old girl danced behind his eyes, and he pushed it back.

"Well, just come with us anyway. Your parents won't know, and you'd obviously be doing them a favor."

"You don't seriously think I'm letting a little thing like parental approval stand in my way, do you? I'd be out of here like a shot if I could, and I'd just lie to them, no big deal -'Oh yeah, I must have been at the library when you called, I got so much accomplished, Mother, you would be truly thrilled.' But I have no money, none. They've got me on a 'generous allowance' Bob's exact words -- which means I can't even afford a decent vacation."

"Didn't they give you a credit card?"

"No. They don't even trust me with a piece of plastic. 'Money doesn't grow on trees,' and 'you won't appreciate the value of money if you don't earn it yourself' -- those are more Bobisms, he's damned William Shakespeare."

"And he seems to have a bizarre obsession with trees," Phillip observed.

Chris didn't bother to smile. "It's not like they don't have enough, they must be loaded. They paid off our house years ago, he's vice president of Fort Knox, I'm their only kid, and now my mom's working too.

And I know they've had all these Merrill Lynch accounts stacked up for my college career since I was three years old. They're just stingy old fools. It's not like they have any fun with the money. I mean, what's it for, to admire? That's meaningless. And it's just not the way things are done these days, they're such old farts."

"Well, you'll have the last laugh when you're seventy-five and they drop dead and leave it all to you. Then you can really have a blast." Phillip stood up and stretched. "They're not the types to leave it to some cat-and-dog hospital are they?"

"No, I'm sure they'll want their grand line to continue. So, when I'm eighty, I can move into the Kenilworth manse. Terrific. I hate that dump."

"Yup. They'll probably have it all handicap-ready for you. Really, it's too bad you can't get your hands on some of it sooner. I'm lucky. My parents have no principles."

Chris didn't say anything. He cradled an empty beer bottle and looked depressed. Phillip stood up and patted him roughly on the shoulder.

"Don't worry, it'll be okay. Hey, we're way late for dinner. Why don't you grab your coat, and we'll get a pizza."

"No thanks. I've got an hourly tomorrow, I suppose I should study."

"So what're you going to do, about spring break, I mean? You can't stay here. I don't even know if they keep the heat on, and I don't want to be sitting on some 85 degree beach, my toes in the warm sand, watching the senoritas, and then suddenly have the image of you flash by, in this frozen garret with your hands in those

18

fingerless gloves and your teeth chattering. It might spoil an otherwise perfect moment for me."

"I don't know. Maybe I'll drive back to Chicago and hang out with some guys I know at Northwestern. I could drop in on my parents too, give them a little surprise. There must be some way to gouge more money out of them."

"You're a prince, Chris. Well, they did give you a great car." Phillip paused to savor a vision of the shiny red Fiero.

"The prize for straight A's in all five of my honors courses junior year. Nothing is without its price, my friend."

"Yup, and no good deed goes unpunished. Hey, we're starting to sound like Bob. Must be the beer." Phillip slung on his down jacket and headed for the door. "Want anything from the pub?"

"No thanks. Hey, have you seen my dissecting kit?"

"No, and I wish you'd keep track of it. I don't want to walk to the toilet one night and find it in my foot. That thing scares me."

"Don't worry, Phillip. Nothing escapes me for long. And I only hurt people on purpose."

Chapter Two

Saturday, April 6, 1996

Plopped at the dinette in her Skokie bungalow, Meredith Bennett, under-employed Assistant State's Attorney and divorced mother of two, flipped to the political cartoons in the Saturday morning *Trib* and cracked a grin over her tepid coffee. Turning the page to the engagement announcements, she paused. Now, at her ex-husband Dr. Alexander Bennett's house in Kenilworth, her daughters, Maggie and Lucy, ages eleven and nine, were undoubtedly ensconced in the new, improved Mrs. Bennett's designer kitchen before the world's most fabulous breakfast.

"Mom, she gets the best chocolate doughnuts, they come in a white box and they have these little crumb things on them, and she lets us drink Diet Coke with them, unless Dad's there, and then she gives us milk. No offense, Mom, but those Wheaties you get are gross."

Which led to her usual alternate-Saturday-morning question: should she, Meredith Bennett, dogged prosecutor of shoplifters and the odd Class X felon, and derelict (for engaging in said dogging) mother of Maggie and Lucy, further deprive her daughters of her maternal influence by leaving them for an additional hour with the nubile Mrs. Bennett Part II, who would toss them a bowl of sugar cubes and plop them in front of Smurf cartoons - - or should she pick them up before she went to the grocery store and subject herself to moans for cookie cereals? Shawna wouldn't care.

"Sure, Meredith," she would say, "we're just hanging out here (munching sugar cubes), it's no big deal either way."

Meredith supposed she was lucky. Shawna was kind to Maggie and Lucy, and they enjoyed her company while their father played the dashing cardiologist with numerous Nordstrom's bills to pay. But listening to her daughters idolize the teenybopper who had stolen her husband was Meredith's idea of an emetic. Although, after ten years, her marriage had been of the old shoe variety, Meredith had been fond of it. She had loved her husband, and sometimes she was afraid she still did.

Scuffing across the linoleum in terrycloth house slippers that looked like something her grandmother would have unearthed from the back of her closet, Meredith rinsed her cereal bowl and turned off the coffeemaker. It was relaxing here alone after a week of court calls and motions and schlepping children to piano lessons and begging them to take showers. But it was also eerily quiet. She tripped over the shag carpet into her avocado bathroom and checked her face in the medicine cabinet mirror. Yup, she was still forty-one. Her hair was still a fuzzing, curly brown with silver strands, her eyes were still near-sighted behind gold rimmed glasses, and she was now seven pounds overweight, up from the five she had decided to accept as endearing shortly before Alexander dumped her for Shawna three years ago.

Slipping on her sneakers and her comfy down jacket, Meredith decided to visit her old Jewel grocery store, on the Wilmette-Kenilworth border, alone. The kids would be happier in their vegetative state, and she would spend less money on pop tarts and aspirin. She and Maggie and Lucy could rebond while they put away all the yucky food she had bought.

Meredith drove her Honda into a handy parking space between a black BMW and a red Mercedes convertible. Despite the obvious risk that some North Shore predator might swipe her Andrew Lloyd Webber tapes, she decided to be wild and leave the car unlocked. She picked her way through abandoned shopping carts and the giant hibiscus sale, stomped on the automatic door pad, and entered the world of food.

Thirty minutes later, her cart brimming with double fudge brownie ice cream and goldfish crackers, Meredith noticed a familiar blonded head stooped over the bananas. The woman snapped two off a bunch and glanced up guiltily.

"Suzanna, how are you?" Meredith hadn't seen her former neighbor, Suzanna Healey, in a couple of years, and she was genuinely pleased.

"I'm fine, thanks. I haven't seen you in a long time. How are you, how are the girls?"

"Oh, fine, we're all fine."

This was tedious, and worse, since Meredith felt a closeness to Suzanna, as anyone must who had known her when her daughter died. Catie was five years old, a sweet-faced pixie with white-blonde hair and clear blue eyes. Failing in a moment of reckless dash to make a tight turn on Oxford Street, a teenage driver had killed her as she chalked pink tulips on the sidewalk in front of her house. Meredith would never forget the funeral, the small white casket closed at the front of the chapel, and the family at graveside -- Suzanna red and shaking, Bob clenched, and their thirteen-year-old son Chris standing apart with a few helpless friends, uncomfortable in navy blazers and ties. Suzanna had been raw for months, any gentle inquiry provoking copious tears and apologies. But time had passed, the ballyhooed healing process had presumably done its work, and walls had been re-erected.

"So." Meredith tried again. "How are you?"

"Oh, fine, thanks. I have a new job for a health management company. I have to travel a lot, but it's exciting. Chris is at Princeton, you know."

"Well, that's great. Does he like it?" Meredith asked.

"Oh, yes, he's doing great. And how are the girls? Do they like school in -- where are you -- Skokie?"

"They like it as much as kids do. It seems to be a good school system," Meredith said, feeling as if she were chewing. "Maggie's eleven now, and Lucy's nine. We're getting along fine, though it's a little lonely for me sometimes. I'm trying to handle an occasional serious crime, after dodging them for so many years in order to spend more time with the kids. You get tired of jay-walkers after a while."

"Yes, I suppose you do. Well, nice to see you," Suzanna said. "We should get together for lunch sometime."

23

"That would be nice. Happy fruit shopping."

"Right." Suzanna smiled. "You too."

So, here they were, two adult women who had lived within a few hundred feet of each other for years, each with her own tragedies and passions, and all they could do was grin and nod, like a couple of plaster dogs with spring heads boinging in the back of a car. Well, at least she had complained a little. Meredith flung a few bananas into her cart and headed to the checkout line. She wondered how Suzanna really liked tugging on stockings at seven a.m. every day and driving to Kenosha to talk to cheese makers about their employee hospitalization coverage. She wondered whether Chris was learning anything, and how much trouble he got into, and how much Suzanna missed him. And she wondered whether Bob, the stiff-suited banker, ever kissed her or surprised her or smacked her around. But she would never know these things, because it wouldn't be polite to ask, and it wouldn't be appropriate to tell.

Meredith loaded the groceries into the trunk of her car, turned the Phantom up loud, and chugged north on Sheridan Road. The crisp April air glittered off the icy lake, while black, leafless branches split the sky into puzzle pieces. Meredith turned left onto Kenilworth Avenue, then right onto Warwick.

The new Bennett abode was, as the realtors crowed, convenient to lake, transportation, and schools, not that the last two were the least bit relevant. Meredith could not imagine the groovy Shawna waiting patiently for a bus, or a cane-wielding Alexander stumbling up the stadium steps for the high school graduations of Shawnette, Shawn, and the Shawntels. Alex might have

24

married the girl, he did marry her, but he wouldn't actually procreate with her.

The Honda putted to a stop in front of the cottage-on-steroids. Meredith felt a pang whenever she saw it, because she knew Alexander would never have chosen it, and yet he had bought it for his bride. It was peach stucco, with a steeply pitched, shimmering tile roof, a wicker porch swing, and trellises for the roses which Meredith would have killed instantly if she had attempted them herself. The brown-green spring grass covered a half acre of yard, neatly contained within a mercifully nonwhite, weathered picket fence. The house acted as a barometer of Meredith's psychological condition, provoking either giggles or watery gloom. Before her vapid conversation with Suzanna, Meredith might simply have smirked as she walked up the stone path, but now she marched forward grimly. Well, she had to rescue Hansel and Gretel from the candy cottage, whether she wanted to confront the witch or not.

She rang the doorbell, and after a moment, to her surprise, Alexander answered it. He was tall and extravagantly thin, with tousled brown hair and a careless grin. After three years and all he had done to her, she still felt the school-girl fluttering stomach, overlaid with the adult reality, that he had thrust his fist inside her chest, grabbed her heart, and crushed it.

"Hi. I came for the girls," she said.

"Sure."

He held open the screen door, and she stepped into the foyer, the wardrobe through which she could not pass without his invitation. She was a stranger now, a guest in his home.

"They had a lot of fun," he said. "I was late last night, but I understand they had pizza and watched a couple videos. This morning we had breakfast together. They like my pancakes," he said, blushing.

"I know."

Meredith made lousy pancakes. She rushed and turned the burner up too high, and they were brown on the outside and raw in the middle. But Alexander was meticulous and patient. He didn't make his pancakes with love exactly, but he made them with care. Which was one reason Shawna had been such a shock.

"Here they are. Oh."

The family room had a vaulted ceiling, the inverse of the roof peaks outside, white and pink and gold, a fairy dwelling. Alexander's three girls sat clustered in the center of the couch, Shawna in the middle, with Maggie and Lucy flanking her like the leaves of a flower.

"Can we see the one of you smushing cake into Daddy's mouth? That's my favorite," said Maggie.

"I love your wedding dress, it's so satiny, and I like those little pearl things. I want to look just like you when I get married," announced Lucy.

"You will," said Shawna. "Look, here's smushing and the dress, all in one shot. Doesn't he look goofy with that frosting on his nose?"

"Mag, Luce, your mom's here," said Alexander. "Put that thing away."

Maggie shut the book and thrust it onto the corner of the table farthest away from Meredith. Maggie looked guilty, Alexander looked distressed, even little Lucy shifted uncomfortably, and Meredith was in pain. The only one who appeared completely unperturbed was

Shawna. And why not? It was no secret that Shawna and Alexander were married. Of course they had a wedding album, through which they would occasionally browse. Why, then, did facing a few frozen moments hurt so much? Meredith looked at Alexander, and he met her eyes. She wasn't crazy. He felt it too. Somehow, seeing the tangible evidence of that ritual was more than she should be expected to bear. He touched her shoulder.

"It doesn't matter," she said.

"I know. Come on. We'll wait for the kids out here." And together, for a moment, they turned their backs on his wife.

"Why are you loading the guns?"

A bag of apples and chicken breasts balanced on her right hip and a gallon of skim milk dangling from her left index finger, Suzanna struggled in through the back storm door, while Bob, unmoved on the mudroom floor, calmly cleaned and loaded his pistols. Suzanna hated the guns, and Bob's fascination with them had always unnerved her. Once, long ago, Bob had tried to include her in his hobby. He had dragged her to gun shows in collar counties and spent hours extolling fluted barrels and inlaid stocks and powder flasks. But Suzanna was alternately bored and repulsed, and Bob had finally released her to the perennial garden and the manicurist. With the advent of the children, she had insisted that he lock the guns in a cabinet in his study, but now he had taken to keeping several revolvers in an open rack in the mudroom, where he polished and fondled and generally admired them. And although he never mentioned it, and she didn't ask, Suzanna thought he took some of them out occasionally and actually fired them.

But she had always told him clearly that she did not want loaded weapons in the house. According to the newspaper, guns were far more likely to be shot accidentally, or deliberately in a domestic dispute, than to protect the family from an intruder. And, statistics or not, guns scared her. People's lives were so fragile, so easily and permanently lost.

"I'm just loading them, that's all, cleaning and loading them. Don't worry about it. I'm doing it for you, for your own protection."

Suzanna tripped through to the kitchen and slung the bag and the milk on the table. "What do you mean? I'm not going to use those things."

"Well, you might, you never know. You don't know what you might do in an extreme situation."

Suzanna walked back to the Volvo for two more bags. At least he could set those stupid things down for a minute and help her. She needed that a lot more than some gun she was afraid to pick up. Anyway, nothing ever happened in Kenilworth, and if it did, Bob would protect her. He'd leap at the chance to brandish one of his pistols, like some aging pirate. She struggled back into the mudroom and glared at him.

"What? Look, I'm trying to help you. I just don't like the idea of you here alone at night with nothing to defend you except an emery board."

"You're here, you'll defend me."

Suzanna hoped some thread of playfulness would obscure her growing aggravation. But Bob just continued wiping his guns. All right, fine, she could ignore him too. She finished carrying in the groceries, and with a flounce, shut the door between the mudroom and the kitchen.

What did he mean, when she was alone at night? He had been working late, but he was always home by nine or ten. She certainly wouldn't want to sleep alone here, in this big house, where a roving gang of youths could machete an entire family before the neighbors noticed anything suspicious. Truthfully, even Bob's late nights unnerved her. Sometimes -- she knew it was stupid -- she had a creepy feeling, as if someone were watching her. She would be in the kitchen plunging a teabag into a cup of hot water or upstairs reading on the sitting room sofa, and all of a sudden she would feel someone's eyes on her through the window, staring at her in her robe as she turned a page or stirred a spoon of sugar into her mug. Suzanna didn't tell Bob, she didn't want him to think she was weak and ridiculous, she was supposed to be a sophisticated career woman, for heavens sake. She closed the refrigerator and reopened the mudroom door.

"Bob, it's April 6."

"So what?" he said.

"Well, I thought you might come with me this time. It'd be good for you. And Catie would like it."

"Suzanna, I don't want to go through this again. Catie would not like it. Catie is gone, she doesn't like or dislike anything. And that place, it doesn't mean anything. She's not there. If you get some kind of morbid delight out of driving all the way to hell -- excuse me -- and pretending she is, that's up to you, but I'm going to stay here where I can do something practical."

"Fine. I'll go myself. Do you want me to fix you a sandwich first?"

"I can fix my own sandwich. Have -- whatever it is you have out there."

"Bye."

She went back to the car. There was one grocery bag left, on the front seat. It contained eleven pink roses, a Hershey bar, a pack of bubblegum, and an Archie comic. She climbed in, buckled her seatbelt, took a deep breath, and backed slowly out of the driveway.

Some people are prepared for death. A few, gritting their teeth, even select their own cemetery plots, after carefully considering price, location, respect for the dead, and comfort for the living. But no one could have anticipated Catie's death, and Bob and Suzanna had to scramble to come up with a proper place. The only local cemeteries Suzanna could think of at the time were Memorial Park in Skokie, near Marshall Fields, and Calvary, on the route downtown, with its austere plaster angels and eerie mausoleums. Calvary was too much for a grieving mother, and Memorial Park, while, with its flat markers and cheery flower arrangements, soothingly in denial, was so much in the midst of life, in the flow of traffic to the mall. Bob finally settled on Eternity Gardens in Downer's Grove, a more remote, grassy setting, where an oak tree would shade Catie's resting place. But, as she slogged the fifty-five minutes of jam-packed expressway, Suzanna sometimes wished they had picked a closer spot. She might have liked to drop in on Catie casually, on her way to buy new sandals or after eating oriental chicken salad with a friend. This way, the visit seemed so much more monumental and upsetting.

Eventually, Suzanna turned in at the wrought iron gates, past the guard station, and toward Catie's oak. After parking on the roadside, she retrieved her Jewel bag and approached the leafless tree. Her toes touched the marker, "Catherine Healey, 1985-1990, Beloved Angel Child." Surprisingly, Bob had written that last. After her burial, he had turned to stone.

Suzanna knelt and touched the cold brass, and a chilly breeze stirred her hair. She removed the candy bar, the gum, the comic book, and finally, the eleven roses, and laid them carefully across the grave.

"Happy birthday, Catie," she whispered, and she sank onto the cold grass and started to cry.

After six years, it still hurt. But she would not neglect her own daughter, her baby girl. Catie would have wanted her to visit, she would have enjoyed these tokens. And she wouldn't be a child much longer. What would Mom bring her next year, maybe a pair of earrings and a Hootie and the Blowfish cassette. Suzanna smiled slightly and wiped her eyes.

Maybe this summer she could get Chris to come out here again. Catie would like that, she had looked up to him so much, her big brother. And it wasn't his fault, what had happened, nor her fault either, though they couldn't help blaming themselves sometimes, and she knew Bob still blamed them both. She was gone for twenty minutes, Chris was in the house, in charge, and when she got home the police were in the front yard, and their daughter was dead.

Suzanna placed both her palms flat on the ground, on top of her child's grave. Are you all right, she thought, are you cold, are you afraid? She remembered the tiny coffin with Catie inside, in her sparkly party shoes, with her special blanket and her stuffed bear, and a good wool blanket to keep her warm. All that was here, just six feet away from her hands, but it was a world away, and she refused to imagine what it looked like now. She would think of Catie in the sky, watching her, telling her not to worry, that she was safe and happy and free, and that some day, they would be together again. That is what she would believe.

Suzanna stood. She smoothed her skirt and brushed off her hands.

"Bye, Catie. We love you. I'll be back in a few weeks, but you're always with me, you're always in my thoughts."

She whispered that, though she knew it wasn't quite true after six years. But when Suzanna came here, it all came rushing back. And she needed that, in a way. She felt it was right.

Seeing the dark, familiar house made him want to wretch -- the boring white fake Colonial front, the pretentious columns, the decapitated shrubs under the living room windows, and the front porch light always gleaming for someone who would never show up. It was Saturday night, but Chris doubted his parents were out carousing, or even at a PG movie. They would be in the back of the house, in the fabulous family room addition, Bob mutely absorbed in a basketball game, and Suzanna fidgeting beside him, in a vain attempt to have some company, however inert. Chris parked his red Fiero on the street in front, in case he needed to make a quick getaway. He shut off its lights and stepped out. He could get his suitcase later, in the unlikely event that he decided to stick around.

He considered ringing the front doorbell, but he couldn't see any signs of life, and sometimes you couldn't hear the bell over the T.V. Anyway, this was his house too. He walked around the locked garage to the back door. Propping the screen door with his shoulder, Chris slid the backdoor key, which, for some inexplicable reason he still kept on the ring with his car and dorm keys, into the lock. He turned it and the knob a hard right, and the door popped open. The mudroom was still immaculate, no yipping dogs with grimy paws to liven up this morgue. Dear Old Dad's gun collection seemed to be creeping downstairs. Three pistols perched on a rack opposite jackets hanging on hooks, like in some imitation English manor house. Chris remembered when he was little, standing in the study staring at the rows of shiny guns locked in the glass display case. A couple of times, Bob had taken Chris, His Son, to a shooting range, and Bob had showed him how to load and aim and fire. That was B.C.D., Before Catie Died, a different era entirely. For a few months A.C.D., Chris would lie awake at night, listening for the pop of the cabinet lock, and wondering if Bob would shoot Chris or Suzanna or himself. But he never heard it. Instead, Bob took all the anger and all the tenderness he had ever felt and walled them up inside himself. Or maybe he kept them in canopic jars buried in the basement, like some eviscerated mummy.

Chris eased open the mudroom door and tiptoed into the kitchen. God, it was magnificent, it just took his breath away. Five years ago, Suzanna had thrown herself into home remodeling. She had wanted to move, but Bob wouldn't allow it. "It's only a house, there's no point in running away from it," he said, even though Suzanna begged him, swearing that every time she saw the front sidewalk, she relived that horror all over again. Instead, she dug up the back of the house, the cozy kitchen where Catie used to listen to her Rice Krispies, and the sunroom where she kept her Barbies in bins next to the T.V. And Bob was pleased, the granite kitchen and paneled family room were so much more bank executive than the house's previous incarnation. He and Suzanna ran into trouble again upstairs.

The architect urged them to build a master bedroom suite -- not that they would use the sitting room or jacuzzi, but as a good investment, a line of reasoning which easily persuaded Bob. But, in order to make the second floor work, they really needed to gut that empty small bedroom next to their old bedroom and turn it into a bathroom. Catie's pink carpet would be ripped up, the floor covered with gray marble, and a shower with variously arranged nozzles installed where her bed used to be. Suzanna cried, this was going too far, they didn't need a fancy bathroom. It was only a room, Bob said, it might as well be put to its highest financial use, Suzanna needed to pull herself together. And every time Chris passed that slick bathroom, he remembered the pink ruffled bed, and he shrieked inside.

He could hear the T.V. drone, he had been right, they were here, just a few feet away. But now he knew he had made a mistake in coming, he couldn't face the house, he couldn't face his parents. Suddenly, the kitchen light turned on.

34

"My God, you gave me a shock! Chris, I didn't know you were coming home. How are you, Dear? Did you drive? You must be exhausted."

His mother's slippered feet scurried across the tile, and her slight arms flung around him. She was so little compared to him, as if they had switched places and now she was the child. He pulled away.

" I'm okay."

"Well, come and see your father. Bob, look who's here! Oh, he'll never hear us, you know how he is when he's watching the Bulls."

Reluctantly, Chris followed his mother through the French doors into the cavernous family room, designed to resemble an estate library, but without the books. In the built-in bookcases Suzanna displayed a Steuben glass dolphin, an elaborate vase loaded with silk flowers, photographs of a prepubescent Chris and Catie, and a few forlorn hardcover bestsellers which she must have received as gifts.

"Bob." She stood in front of the T.V. "Look who's here."

"At this hour?" He turned, and he saw Chris, and he actually stood up and smiled. "How are you, Son? We weren't expecting you. So, you decided to come home for spring break."

"Well, you might say the decision was thrust upon me. It was that or stay in the dorm and freeze my ass off."

Bob frowned. Suzanna stepped over and took Chris's arm.

"Come on, Dear. There's some cold chicken in the fridge, and some leftover salad. I'll fix you a late supper, and then you can get to bed."

Hale the conquering hero, the great Princetonian they lived to brag about. This is what he got in real life, cold leftovers, and then exile to his room with the airplane wallpaper and the lonely twin bed. He thought about Phillip and Derek in Cancun, sipping margaritas with little umbrellas and stretching their arms in the hot southern sun. A chill hung in the Kenilworth house, like a grave.

"I'm not tired. Christ, Mother, quit treating me like I'm five years old." He stopped, and they both turned white. "And can't somebody turn up the heat in here? You must have to break the ice in the toilet bowl."

"Look, Mister." Bob moved to the doorway. "I know you're ticked off because we didn't foot the bill for that Mexican junket, but that's no way to talk to your mother."

"It's all right, Bob, he's just had a long day." Suzanna concertedly reached for items in the refrigerator and set them on the counter.

"Ticked off, as you so quaintly put it, doesn't begin to describe how I feel about this vacation. All I wanted was a little fun, and it's not like you don't have the money. I work hard, I perform, you can't say I haven't come through for you with the big name college bumper sticker. So don't I deserve a little payback, just a break now and then?"

"Look, I don't want to go through this again." Chris could see his father's knuckles, bony white as they gripped the back of a kitchen chair. "If you want to go to Mexico and get thrown in some jail for the next decade, that's your business, but you're footing the bill. You expect me to give you my hard-earned money so you can go drinking and screwing and God knows what else, on top of the $30,000 a year which I fork over for Princeton, which I am happy to do, but it's a hell of a lot of money, and you don't seem to appreciate it. I'm trying to teach you the value of a dollar, and I'm also trying to protect you in some small way, though I know you're a big, tough guy, and you don't want any protection. Frankly, your mother's already lost one child, and I don't think she could stand to go through it again."

"Don't push this off on her, you don't care about her. And don't push it off on that."

Chris looked at his mother. She had set a bluebird placemat on the table, with a napkin folded in a triangle, a silver knife, fork, and spoon, a tall glass of milk, and a stoneware plate with two chicken breasts, salad, and a slice of French bread. Now she just stood there, her eyes welling.

"Please, Bob, it's okay. I think he understands."

Chris turned on her. "And don't you speak for me. You're always trying to make nice and pacify this jerk. He's never liked me, he doesn't want to make me happy, he just wants to use me. He's got gobs of money, and he just can't stand the idea that anybody might enjoy it. You must be freezing, what do you have, two sweaters on, and he won't even turn up the stupid heat, that's how much he cares about your feelings. He's selfish, that's all." He turned to Bob. "I asked you, I groveled for God's sake, but you wouldn't listen to me, you don't care how I feel or what I want. Well, I'm giving you one more chance. I need more money, and this is not a frivolous thing, I work hard, I need some fun, and you could do this for me with a stroke of the pen." Chris paused. "Please, Dad, Mom. I'm begging you."

37

"Get out." Bob's face was bright red. "I want you out of here now, I don't care if you are my son, I don't care how far you drove. I will continue to foot your college bills, and that is it. And don't come back here until you can show a little gratitude and respect."

"Mom?"

Tears sliding down her cheeks, Suzanna stepped over next to Bob.

"I agree with your father," she forced. "But please - be careful."

"Fine."

Chris turned and marched out of the house. He got into the front seat of his car, rested his forehead on the steering wheel, and cried. Then, he determinedly pulled into a neighbor's driveway and turned around. As he passed the house on his way to Evanston, he averted his eyes, to avoid seeing his mother's face pressed against the upstairs sitting room window. The front porch light was still on. But they obviously weren't waiting for him.

Chapter Three

Tuesday, April 9, 1996

"If the oxygen masks fall, just tighten the straps over your nose and mouth and breathe normally."

From the corner of her eye, Suzanna watched the flight attendant demonstrating the use of the yellow plastic cup attached to a plastic bag that was supposed to save her life if the airplane -- did what depressurized, dropped from the sky? Even imagining the sorts of incidents that might require oxygen was enough to paralyze her, and she doubted that, if she were actually falling, she would have the composure to breathe at all. At least she didn't have to worry about fastening her own mask first, before she helped her panicking child. To her right, Suzanna's boss, Frank Nelson, studied the laminated safety card.

"I think our nearest exit is the window two rows behind us," he whispered, peering over his shoulder.

"I hope it won't come to that. I'm not sure how I'd manage on one of those inflatable slides. I might lose my nerve completely and just stand there gaping at the ground."

"We could go down together," he suggested.

"Like children on the playground. We could make a train."

Suzanna smiled, but Frank frowned. He probably thought she was laughing at him, and she supposed she was. It was comforting, though, having a man so concerned for her welfare. Not that Bob wasn't, of course, if it came to a pinch, but they were used to each other.

"Frank, your presentation today was wonderful," she offered, to make amends. "You're very knowledgeable."

He blushed. "Well, I've been doing this for a long time."

"Still, the terms of the contracts change frequently, and you have such a mastery of them. And you seem so relaxed. I always feel that I'm rummaging through jumbled papers during awkward silences."

"You handled yourself very well, and I'm happy to help, until you get the hang of it. More than happy."

The plane rushed down the runway, and suddenly they were in the air, high above buildings and treetops, in a machine manufactured and inspected by her high school classmates or their equivalents. It didn't bear thinking about. The flight from Detroit to Chicago was only an hour, barely time for a soft drink and a glance through the in-flight magazine. Suzanna reached down to grip the arms of her seat and found that Frank had rested his forearm on the metal stub between them, his hand dangling casually over her knee. Startled, she pulled away.

"Sorry," she said, though she resented the ease with which he had settled into her space. At the same time, she felt the attraction of his maleness, the magnetism which she must fight.

"I have a confession to make," Frank said.

Suzanna looked at him, and she saw the whiskers bristling his cheeks and the lines of wear radiating from the corners of his eyes. And now she had a sense of his nearness, of her confinement with him in this small space, a sense both dreadful and enticing. She knew she should discourage him, stop him now before he embarrassed them both, but at the same time she wondered what he would say. She remained silent, her thin arms clenched across her chest.

"I knew you could handle this trip alone," he said simply, sweat beading his upper lip. "I just wanted to come with you."

"Frank, it's okay. I'm new, I'm glad to have a little more help."

"Yes. Well."

She looked down, and she saw his crude fingers, only inches above her leg.

"Excuse me," she said, unbuckling her seat belt, and she stepped into the aisle. This is silly, she thought, hurrying toward the restroom, he likes you, there's nothing wrong with that, he's a gentleman, nothing will happen. Locked safely in the stall, she sank onto the toilet and put her head in her hands. Once things were so simple. She and Bob had two lovely children, Bob worked and came home and played with them, and at night they watched T.V. together and sometimes they made love. They were content. Now Catie was gone and Chris was terrible, and Bob was barely there, and here she was, on an airplane with a strange, inappropriate man who, she knew, wanted to rub his paws all over her. And that would destroy everything. Her world was held together with scotch tape and paper clips, loosely, but together, and if he touched her, it would blow apart, and she couldn't cope with that.

Locating the kleenex, Suzanna wiped her nose and patted her hair into place. This was only harmless, considerate Frank, she really must get a grip. She and Bob were just in a transition phase, empty-nesters, a new job, Bob turning fifty. In a few months, a year at most, they would be adjusted and content once more. Soon she and Frank would be old pals. He would bounce back from his divorce, discover some spiffy single girl, and Suzanna could invite them both for dinner, or at least coffee and dessert. Frank was going through a transition too, he wasn't used to being alone, but soon he would relax.

Suzanna unlatched the restroom door and stepped carefully back to her seat. Frank appeared to be engrossed in a magazine. She hoped she hadn't upset him with her hasty departure, but she doubted he was that sensitive. Still, he had moved his arm back squarely within the confines of his own space. She slid into her spot and buckled her seat belt loosely, as the flight attendant had instructed.

Glancing at her watch, she saw that they would be landing in only twenty minutes, hardly time to pull out her files or her paperback. Reaching into the seat pouch, she dredged up the flight magazine and turned to the maps in the back. She remembered so little geography, it was always beneficial to review the locations of the different countries in Europe and to take a quick browse through the Caribbean.

That done, she rummaged in the pouch again and pulled out a *Skyshopper*, one of those magazines filled with products that no one could possibly want. Flipping through, she admired the Ceiling Bulb Changer, tongs on a long pole, which might be handy for their family room, the 14-Day Fish Feeder, and the Wrap-Around Neck Massager, which looked a bit threatening, encircling the neck of a blonde woman, her eyes trustingly closed. Amused, she paused at the Chin Gym before discovering a back section entitled, "Safety First." And there he was, on the bottom of the right hand page. The Inflatable Man.

The Inflatable Man was a "life-size, simulated male," created to give strangers the impression that a woman, its owner, was accompanied by a man when she was home alone or driving her car. In various photographs the inflatable man perched in a chair in sporty attire, sat in a window in full business dress, and hilariously deflated into a discreet carrying case. The text noted that clothing was not included, and Suzanna wondered how he looked in the nude, if they had bothered to sculpt in pectoral muscles and a slight crotch bulge, like a Ken doll, or whether he were simply flat and rubbery. He certainly looked real when dressed in sunglasses and a baseball cap and clutching the *Wall Street Journal*, though she doubted that paper was really to his taste. She couldn't imagine stepping out of her Volvo and then casually deflating him, though she thought that her North Shore neighbors would try to pretend it was an everyday occurrence and discreetly avert their eyes. "Ordering is a snap," the magazine promised, and she did look at the price, one hundred dollars, rather expensive, plus ten for the pump, which you probably needed.

"We are now making our final preparations for landing," the flight attendant announced over the loud speaker.

Smiling, Suzanna glanced over at Frank, dozing with his tray table safely stowed. She closed her copy of *Skyshopper*, and, for reasons unclear to her, slipped it into her briefcase.

Frank rummaged in his wallet for the fifteen dollar cab fare from the airport. He was sure he had a twenty, but now he couldn't find it, and the cabby was a burly Arab whom Frank did not want to cross. Finally he counted up his ones, and two fives, fifteen bucks exactly, but he could only scrounge up forty-two cents for a tip. He thrust the wad through the window, grabbed his briefcase, and fled into the lobby.

Frank lived in the ugliest apartment building on the ugliest stretch of Sheridan Road, blocks of faded high rises only inches from four lanes of continuous traffic on and off Lake Shore Drive. The windows of his building bristled at odd angles from its cement walls, as if the whole structure were straining to see beyond the traffic and around the apartment house across the street to the obscured lake. From a distance, this angularity gave the place a skewed, neurotic look. But the price was right, and a C.T.A. bus stopped at its doorstep to deliver Frank downtown. Of course he had his Mazda too, for the drive to his office in the suburbs, but he preferred public transportation in the city.

Frank hurried to the elevator, which creaked up to the fourth floor, and he unlocked his studio apartment. He had everything he needed here, a brown couch that absorbed spills and turned into a bed at night, a dinette with two chairs, just in case, and the room's focal point, a large color T.V. He also had a slot kitchen for heating soup and toasting sandwiches, and a somewhat mildewed bathroom. If Frank had ever had a wife, he would have lived in a larger place, and she would have decorated it with floral curtains and throw pillows. But he had abandoned that hope years ago, after Dinah rejected him. It had taken him a long time to recover, almost fifteen years. His feelings toward Suzanna told him that he had almost done it, though, in bleak moments, the humiliation still recurred.

Frank dropped his briefcase inside the front door and headed into the kitchen to pour himself a bowl of cereal. He had been disturbed by Suzanna's abrupt flight from her airplane seat after he had hinted at his feelings for her, but she seemed relaxed and friendly later, when they walked through the airport together. He had probably overreacted, because of Dinah, and he knew he had to take risks if he wanted Suzanna. Daring, he had offered to treat her to Starbucks and then made light of her refusal -- she had to go home to her husband, she had reported without much enthusiasm. Frank could imagine Bob, an exacting man who demanded that his wife travel a straight line between work and home, who wanted his shirts starched and his pork chops on the table, and who used his money and position as a golden chain to tether Suzanna beside him. To Bob, Suzanna was a maid, a companion at dinner parties, and a symbol of conservative family values. Despite the absence of love between them, Bob would never let her go without an enormous fight.

Stirring his Cheerios into a bowl of milk, Frank plopped onto the couch and stared at the T.V. screen. He had started loving Suzanna practically the moment he saw her, when she had stepped into his office for her job interview in her pink suit, clutching her purse as if it were a prop. She held her head high, her smile composed, but when he took her hand to shake it, it felt soft and trembly and fine. He didn't meet many women like Suzanna in his business, they were mostly redheads with beehives and skirts showing a lot of beefy leg. Suzanna had a vulnerable elegance which captivated him. She had admitted that she hadn't worked in a long time, but he could tell she was smart and eager to learn.

Normally, he didn't fraternize with his employees, but Suzanna was an exception. He hadn't meant to lie to her, to make up that story about his recent divorce, it really wasn't such a great idea, since anyone could tell her that he had never been married at all. But she didn't seem to chat with the other women, they had so little in common, she was in another class. And he had thought that if he told her, she would soften towards him and trust him a little, and he had been right. She didn't speak much about her own husband, a lady would keep her complaints private when talking to a man, but the look on her face told him that any passion she had felt had long since passed, that the only thing she could feel toward Bob now would be responsibility, and maybe even disgust.

46

And Frank could sense Suzanna's attraction to him. He was considerate and protective, and she responded to that, though her natural reserve and her married state kept her at arm's length. Frank didn't blame Suzanna for playing it safe and sticking with her rich banker husband, for letting her feminine dependence overshadow her need for love. But he knew that, if Bob were out of the picture, she would rush into his arms. It was so hard to wait. Restless, he stretched, set his bowl in the kitchen sink, and went out the front door. He would take his usual drive. That would make him feel better.

Suzanna handed the cab driver twenty-six dollars. Ever since they had entered Wilmette, she had been calculating the tip, twenty percent of the metered fare. At Kenilworth Avenue she opened her purse and pulled the bills from her wallet. She held them ready until the man pulled into her driveway.

"Thank you very much," she said firmly.

"Thank you, Ma'am. Do you need any help with anything?"

"No, I'm fine. Have a good night."

She stepped from the cab with her briefcase and purse and closed the back door. The porch light was on as usual, but the house looked dark and empty. That was strange, it was almost nine o'clock, but maybe Bob had taken advantage of her absence to work later than usual. She pulled the key from her purse, fumbled with the front door lock, stepped into the hallway, and bolted the door behind her. The answering machine on the kitchen desk beeped sporadically, an irritation and a comfort. Perhaps that was Bob, explaining himself. Suzanna imagined returning to a warmly lit house, a husband rushing to the door to kiss her hello, taking her briefcase, leading her to the kitchen for a candle-lit late supper and then straight up to bed. Well, that was a dream, not even a wife would do all that.

She turned on the lights, hung her trench coat in the closet, slipped off her shoes, and padded across the oak floor to the kitchen. Bob had left the window open a crack, and she shut it and turned the inadequate latch. Maybe she should invest in a home security system, or at least in a sign claiming that they had one. She had always disliked the fortress mentality cropping up among neighborhood newcomers, but that was when she could afford to, when she had a teenaged son in the house, and a husband who came home for dinner.

She flipped on the kitchen lights and immediately felt exposed. Anyone in the backyard could see her now, darting between appliances, as if she were on stage in a very dull play. She pushed the message button on the answering machine and stepped back, away from the window.

The first message was a hang-up, nothing but fuzz and a beep, probably a sales person, hopefully not Chris wanting to talk and then thinking better of it. Next came Bob's tight, steady voice. He sounded as if he were reading a script.

"Suzanna, I am sorry to tell you this way. I thought it would be easier if I cleared out when you were gone. I have rented an apartment for myself in the city, and I moved into it today. I have taken some of my clothes, and I will get the rest of my things soon, when I have time. Don't worry, you can have the house and most of the furniture, I'll only want a few basics. I think you have to admit that I saw you and Chris through, and now that you are both independent, it is time for me to think of myself. I don't have a phone yet, so if you need to get in touch with me, you can call me at the bank. I'm sorry if this is a shock, but you're a smart woman, I'm sure you've had your suspicions. Goodbye."

The answering machine clicked and then resumed its insistent beep. Bob had left her. It didn't seem possible. Their marriage wasn't perfect, but how could he do this, how could he leave her alone after all these years? Her stomach grabbed, and she ran to the bathroom and heaved up coffee-colored phlegm over the toilet bowl. She wet a towel and wiped her mouth and her whole face, beige streaky make-up and powder eye shadow and black mascara staining her good peach guest towel. To hell with it, what did it matter now? She sank onto the floor, the cold marble somehow comforting in its clarity. What could she do? She couldn't be alone in this echoing house. She thought of calling Chris, he could come and be with her, but he had stomped out in a huff three days ago and she didn't even know where he was. Besides, he was her child, he would be upset and need her support, and he had to go to school. She had neighbors of course, but it was late, they had children to mind, they were probably in bed. And how could she tell her friends what had happened to her, it was so humiliating, her husband had left, he had rented an apartment for God's sake, he must have had a girlfriend for months, and she didn't have a clue. Her parents were

49

dead, and her brothers lived far away, and they had their own families to support. Frank flitted into her consciousness, but she immediately pushed him back, it wasn't right, she was married, he was her boss, he wasn't her style, he was just a complication. She was completely alone, and she would have to cope alone, but she couldn't, she didn't know how.

Tentatively she stood, and she saw her bloodless reflection, the lines around her eyes and mouth, the face which she had oiled and clarified and moisturized from the hairline to the throat in a futile attempt to stay young for Bob. Suzanna saw the still blue dazzle of her eyes and the creases mapping the history of their love and losses, her life's education, perhaps even an enhancement, she had thought hopefully, her face reflecting hard won grace and wisdom. But no, all Bob could see was what was missing, the smooth, naive surface, fibers taut with lack of use, the exuberance and plain animal sexiness of youth. Suzanna grabbed handfuls of hair and she pulled, remembering the hours, consolidated as weeks, that she had spent sitting in a chair while a woman pulled strands through a rubber cap or wrapped them in foil, so that she would be blonde again. Her eyes filled, wet with pain, and she took her forehead, its one deep crease and the other smaller ones, her pasty, unlovable, aged face, and she smacked it against the plaster wall again and again and again.

She didn't stop until the pain flashed, and she opened her eyes and saw the translucent red smear above the light switch. She found herself in the mirror, eyes puffed and bubbling, her forehead bruised and split inside out. She must stop, she was hurting herself, and people would see and wonder, and she couldn't have that. Suzanna reached for the other peach towel, and she wet it. First, she wiped the wall, carefully removing the garish smear. Then, she touched it to her forehead, dabbing the gash and shivering. She must get hold of herself. She could pretend, she could fool herself, she could try. Bob was working late and would be home after she was asleep, she could just imagine that. A nice hot bath would relax her after travelling, and then bed. Suzanna double-checked the front and back doors and then picked up her briefcase and carried it up to the master bedroom suite. But she found that she couldn't strip off her clothes and sink naked into a deep, warm tub, alone in the house as she was. Her suit jacket came off, and that was as far as she could go. What if someone came into the house? She stood at the bedroom window, staring blankly into the darkness. She could swear she felt someone watching her.

All night, Suzanna swept from room to room, switching on lights to reassure herself, then turning them off so that she could gaze outside unobserved. Finally, at five a.m., she curled under an afghan on the sitting room couch and dozed. At seven, she rose, showered, and dressed for work. Fumbling through her briefcase, her fingers closed on the *Skyshopper* magazine, which had seemed so ludicrous only a few hours ago. She couldn't spend another night like her last one. She hesitated only a moment. Then she removed her credit card from her wallet, dialed the 800 number, and placed her order.

Chapter Four

Wednesday, April 10, 1996

"Suzanna, what happened to you?"

She walked calmly into his office, but her hand travelled involuntarily to her head, as Frank leaped up and shut the door. Suzanna had hoped that the make-up and blonde fringe she had arranged this morning would adequately conceal her wound.

"I fell, that's all, I slipped and bumped myself on the kitchen counter. Silly really, clumsy -- it looks worse than it is. If you have time, I wanted to ask you a few questions before my trip next Monday."

"Of course, please sit down." Frank looked uncomfortable, but apparently he had decided not to press her. He walked around to his chair and punched the intercom button. "Brenda could you bring us some coffee? And one of those nice sweet rolls you brought, for Suzanna."

Relieved, Suzanna settled herself across from Frank. She was nervous and exhausted, but at least while she was in the office, Frank would take care of her.

"Men are so lucky. They get to eat dessert."

Treena gazed amorously at the slice of chocolate cream pie which Bob had thoughtlessly flung onto his cafeteria tray. Her tossed salad with low fat Italian dressing would net her a tinier dress size, but Bob, loaded up with mostaccioli, garlic bread, the pie, and a real coke, seemed a sultan of self-indulgence. As a high-level male, he had the luxury of camouflaging his paunch behind a dark suit coat and an air of self-importance, while Treena, the subordinate female, had to live, at least in part, by her waistline.

"Don't be fooled, it tastes like chocolate shaving cream, with an indefinite shelf life. In fact, I think I recognize this very slice from last Christmas." Bob smiled. "And you could certainly eat it too. I don't know what you're worried about. If you're good, I'll give you a bite."

"You've got yourself a deal," Treena said, as they walked together to the nearest cashier. Bob was certainly feeling chipper today. "And thanks for your words of comfort." She did have a tiny waist even after two children, she thought with satisfaction, glancing at the array of dumpy women around her. And she knew that her husband Craig and Bob both appreciated her efforts.

"It's on me," Bob said, pulling out his wallet and waving hers back into her purse. As she followed Bob to a quiet table, Treena felt several sets of appreciative male eyes ticking to the swing of her backside. High heels did show her legs to good advantage, and she might as well wear a short skirt while she could. It was businesslike navy after all, and her silk blouse showed just the right amount of smooth white skin. Treena walked a narrow line, enticing, but never sluttish or unprofessional. Somebody in the Snider family had to bring home a decent income, and it wasn't Craig, and brains were a dime a dozen.

Bob and Treena slid into chairs across from each other. She speared a lettuce leaf and lifted it daintily to her lips, as Bob devoured a huge mouthful of cheesy noodles.

"So, what's new with you?" she asked perkily, bending just enough to show deep interest in Bob's every syllable and a good inch of cleavage.

Despite their frequent lunches, Bob had revealed very little of himself to her. Usually, Treena jabbered away, trying to keep someone's voice in the air, and she left the meal hungry and resentful. Still, she must consider these lunches, which Bob obviously enjoyed, part of her job description. She could probably attribute her nice Christmas bonus to them, as well as the perfume Bob had given her, inappropriate perhaps, but worth six months of tedious meals for the effect it provoked in Craig. But now, remarkably, Bob appeared to have something to say.

"Treena, I know the employee cafeteria is not the proper place to discuss this, but -- things have happened -- I have made my move, so to speak -- and I just can't wait any longer."

He set his fork down. This was serious. Treena was fascinated.

"Bob, what is it?" she asked, hoping she looked sympathetic and not simply curious.

"Patience. I will tell you. Please don't say anything until I'm finished."

54

He reached across his tray and took her hand. Alarmed, she glanced around her, but no one seemed to be watching them, so she left it.

"Treena, we have spent a lot of time together during the past year, and you have become more to me than an associate. Day after day, you sit across the desk from me, or across the lunch table, and you are so lovely and young, and I want more than this business relationship -- I can't help it -- and somehow, I feel that you do too."

"Now, Bob, Dear--"

"Don't worry, I'm not about to impugn your honor. I know that we're both married, but these things are not irrevocable. I need you, Treena, and I mean that in the best sense. I want to marry you and take care of you and your daughters. I want to have a real family again. I flatter myself that I am still an attractive man, and I certainly have the financial position and prestige to make you and your children secure. Don't say anything now, I know you're probably surprised, despite our mutual affection, but I think that, once you consider it fully, you will realize that this is really an excellent plan for us all. My son and wife are independent now, they don't need me emotionally or financially. And I might even be able to manage a small stipend for your husband, to further his -- art career." He broke into a broad grin. "I feel so happy now, so relieved. I've wanted to say this to you for a long time."

Treena stared at Bob. Of course she couldn't marry him, it was absurd, he was an old man and she didn't love him and she was already married to Craig, who, granted, had no money, but was amply endowed with other fascinating compensatory attributes. But she needed her job, she didn't want to endanger it. Nor did she want to rip out the small, strange heart that Bob appeared to possess.

"Don't say anything now," he continued. "I know that you have a good analytic mind, and once you consider my proposal carefully -- and it is a proposal, My Dear -- you will recognize its advantages. I do not want to presume anything now, but I believe that, at least in time, you and your girls will come to love me as thoroughly as I love you."

His piece said, Bob tucked vigorously into his remaining carbohydrates. Treena watched him, her elderly boss, this stranger who had grabbed her life in his teeth and was shaking it. In a way, it was funny, and of course flattering, besides being dangerous. At least he had given her time to stall, to figure out what to say. Apparently her charms were more potent than she had thought. Considering the perfume gift's testosterone-raising effect, she could hardly wait to go home and tell Craig about this.

"I'll have that bite of pie now," she said, and she coyly licked her lips.

When Craig finally emerged from his studio, the spare bedroom which was only spare because he insisted that his creative urges take precedence over their daughters' need for privacy, Treena was chopping cucumbers and waiting for water to boil. She had stripped off her suit and stockings and pulled on her ripped jeans and one of Craig's v-neck tee shirts. Her blonde hair loose on her shoulders, her face make-up free, and her feet bare, she had transformed herself from bank executive to Bohemian painter's wife, like a snake shedding its tight skin.

"Mommy, what's for dinner?" asked Ellie, snatching a handful of cucumbers. "Doris never lets us have a snack, and I'm dying."

"Well, Doris is right, you should eat a good dinner," Treena said doubtfully, wondering what other arbitrary restrictions the babysitter had imposed and then pushing the idea from her mind. They needed Doris, whatever the future cost in psychoanalysis. "Oh, Craig, you're down, good. We'll eat in about ten minutes."

"Ten minutes," moaned Ellie, grabbing her stomach.

"Go find your sister and play something. You can color that book I brought you about saving your money. I'll call you when it's ready, it won't be long. So, did you have a good day?" she asked Craig casually, breaking lettuce into bite-sized pieces.

"Not really. It's so damned frustrating -- the weather's gray, I can't do anything in that squalid little room. Never mind."

Craig labored in chronic unsatisfactory conditions. The light was wrong, the muse had departed, the children were too loud, and how could anyone create Art in a split-level in Buffalo Grove? He spent his days cowering before blank canvases and his nights punishing Treena with his artistic angst. How could she hope to comprehend him, she was a banker for God's sake, all she did was crank out documents day in, day out, no matter the weather or her mood or the state of the children, so that there would be canvases to waste and a

57

boring roof over their heads. Irritated, she turned to see his deep, dark eyes, his thick black hair, and his tall, under-nourished frame -- he was the only person she had ever known who actually forgot to eat. And truly, he asked very little of her, though he did enjoy sleeping inside and the odd can of baked beans. The children, who required a much larger financial investment, had been her idea.

"Craig, I'm sorry." Treena ran her damp hands over his arms. "It's almost May, the rain has to stop soon. Waiting for summer is always hard."

"Cut it out." Craig yanked himself away from her. "Jesus, I'm not your infant, I don't need you to soothe me. So, what great deeds did you accomplish today?"

She decided to ignore the sneer. The water was boiling, and she spilled a box of stiff spaghetti into it.

"Not much, the usual forms and phone calls. I had lunch with Bob Healey today."

"Yeah? What did that vermin want?"

Craig had met Bob at a New Year's party at the Healeys' house last year, and he had not been impressed, particularly when Bob helped Treena out of her holiday cardigan and danced with his hands all over her bare back. The ensuing fuss, including Craig's drunken attempt to punch Bob in the gut, had almost cost Treena a promotion. Although it had netted her a jealous, territorial predator on their living room floor later that night.

"Actually, he asked me to marry him."

"What? You're kidding."

"Honestly, he seemed to be serious." She turned away and stirred the spaghetti. "He told me that he wanted to marry me and make a family with me and the girls."

Treena could feel Craig behind her, and she could swear the kitchen was ten degrees warmer. Suddenly, she felt his fingers digging into her upper arms.

"And what exactly did you say?"

"Ouch, Craig, you're hurting me. I told him -- well, nothing, he told me not to say anything, and I didn't know what to tell him. I mean, obviously I'll say no, but I didn't want to get him all upset."

"You didn't want to get him upset." Craig twisted Treena around, so that she was facing him. "And what about me?"

"Really, this has nothing to do with you. I want to keep my job, I've got to handle this delicately, so he won't get mad."

"I will not have you swiveling your hips for some old fart who has the hots for you. I'll bet you like this attention, you were just eating it up, weren't you. I can just see you sitting there on his knee, licking your lips."

Treena was not expecting what happened next. She knew that Craig would be violently opposed to the idea of Bob Healey flinging her over his saddle and riding off with her, and she was happily anticipating the forceful sex which normally followed this sort of incident. Lord knew, she hadn't provoked Bob, at least not much, only enough to keep her job and earn a couple of modest bonuses, not enough to make him want to leave his wife of twenty-five years. As Treena glanced over at the boiling pot, she saw Craig's large, sensitive hand rise up, and as she absently noticed how clean it was, as if he hadn't painted for days, the hand swooped down and smacked her hard across the left cheek. The force and the surprise sent her slamming against the stove, her arm against the pot, hot water splashing up onto her shoulder. She screamed.

By the time the children rushed in from the family room, Craig had hauled Treena's arm and shoulder under the faucet and was dousing them with cold water, while she whimpered. Her face felt flushed and swollen, and she knew that if she looked in the mirror, she would see the red print of Craig's hand surrounded by her white, shocked skin.

"It's all right, Girls," Craig said, glancing over. "Mommy just had an accident. Why don't you put on *Snow White*, you like that, while I help her here. Do you know how to work the VCR?"

"Sure. Doris taught us. You okay, Mommy?" Ellie asked.

"Yes, Sweetie, I'm fine. Do what Daddy said, go watch your movie."

"Okay." Ellie scampered back to the family room, with Janie behind her.

After a few minutes, Craig turned off the faucet and pulled Treena upright. He found a fresh dish towel and gently mopped her shoulder.

"Are you okay?" he asked. With his fingertip, Craig touched her blistered arm, and then her pink, puffy cheek.

"Yeah, I'm okay."

"I'm sorry. But -- it's not all my fault, you were trying to get a rise out of me. But I didn't mean to hurt you, Treena, I swear it. I just couldn't stand the thought of you and that guy."

"I know. But I had to tell you. I couldn't keep something like that a secret. Then it would be as if I were colluding with him, and I'm not. I'm married to you. But you have to promise never to do that again, I mean it. There's a line, Craig, and you crossed it."

She shivered. They looked down and saw that her tee shirt was completely soaked.

"I could enter a contest."

"Yeah, you could." Carefully, he took his index finger and traced the outline of her loose breasts, the tee shirt clinging to them. He started between them, and went around to each side. Finally, he rested his palms against their protruding centers.

"I'm sorry, Treena. I love you. Let's take you upstairs and get you out of these wet things," he said.

"Yes, let's," she said, and their mouths found each other, and their arms went around each others' waists. Melded together, they climbed the split flight of stairs to their bedroom and shut the door.

Afterwards, Treena stood in the bathroom in her polyester bathrobe and brushed her hair. The handprint had faded, and by morning it would be gone. She walked back to the bedroom. Craig sat on the edge of the rumpled sheets, his fists clenched, his eyes staring. She sank down next to him and rested her head on his shoulder.

"What are you thinking?" she asked.

"Nothing. I just hate that guy. I won't let him take you away from me."

"Good." Treena reached up, and she kissed him. "Let's go see if there's anything salvageable in that spaghetti pot."

Chapter Five

Friday, April 12, 1996

On the well-worn couch in their shag-carpeted living room in Skokie, Meredith sat between her daughters, Maggie and Lucy. It was Friday night, and many of Meredith's neighbors were celebrating the advent of the Sabbath Bride with chicken soup and candles and a trip to the local shul. But Meredith, one of the few to display a weak strand of colored lights during December and January, was beginning her ritual day of rest staring at a *Sleeping Beauty* video with her zombified children. Although Maggie and Lucy adored Disney's singing Barbie dolls, Meredith secretly cheered Maleficent, the regal, rejected fairy who cast a vengeful spell over the kingdom and then transformed herself into a particularly scary dragon. Maleficent may have gone a bit far, but she was a powerful wronged woman, a far better role model to Meredith than the hopelessly perfect Aurora, whose bland goodness enabled her to charm herbivorous forest creatures.

Meredith yawned and stretched, like a boy on his first date, in order to scratch her daughters' backs. They squirmed with pleasure, their eyes still riveted to the T.V. screen. Meredith felt the worn, familiar fibers of one of Alexander's old U. of C. tee shirts, now Maggie's favorite nightie, and she pushed down the memory of scratching Alex in just this way, and then creeping under the shirt, to his tight, smooth skin.

Alexander was gone. He was with Shawna now. On the screen the shapely blonde princess enticing Prince Charming transformed into Shawna seducing Alexander, her hands lightly touching his, their eyes locked. Meredith would never forget that Friday night four years ago, when Alexander had come to her and begged her to understand. Her and their seven-year-old and their five-year-old.

"You don't have to skulk. I'm still awake."

Meredith propped herself wearily on one elbow and peered through the dim at her husband, returning from the hospital at one a.m. It was December, freezing cold, and the colored lights she and the girls had strung across the front bushes of their Kenilworth home created a weak glow through the translucent bedroom shades. Meredith could see Alexander's face in this light, first sickly green, then blink, a flushed red. And not for the first time, Meredith thought: returning from the hospital -- he said.

"I was reading. I just decided to rest for a minute." She wanted him to know she wasn't sleeping when he was working, as if she needed to prove she wasn't lazy for sleeping at one a.m. after spending her own day slogging in the State's Attorney's office, then making pancakes shaped like mouse heads and playing five thousand games of Candyland to while away a long, lonely evening.

"You don't have to wait up for me," Alexander said. He unbuttoned his shirt and eased the tails out of his pants.

"I know." She paused. "Another emergency?"

"Yes. No. I don't know."

Alexander sat on the edge of the bed and rested his head in his hands. And Meredith thought, oh no, oh my God, oh no. Things are not great now, but it's livable, I can deal with it. Please only let things stay as they are.

"Meredith, I have to tell you --"

"No, you don't. You're tired, we're both tired, it's been a long day. Just come to bed now, you're home now, that's what matters."

She reached out to brush his shoulder, and he sank into her hand, but he said, "No, you don't understand, I can't come to bed. I -- promised I wouldn't."

Meredith pulled back as if he had burned her. She sat straight up, the blankets falling away from the modest flannel nightie she always wore in the wintertime.

"You're right, I don't understand," she said. "You promised me, you married me."

She stumbled out of their bed and stood beside it, her bare feet on the Persian rug covering the beautiful old oak floors of their house, the Bennett family house, Alexander and Meredith and Maggie and Lucy together. She couldn't stay in bed, she felt vulnerable and trapped, a plumped-up matron waiting to be left.

"I know I did, I know. I've done it for ten years. I love you, Meredith, but after a while it just gets old. The life has gone out of it, the joy."

"Do you know how babyish and spoiled you sound? We have two children, two small daughters.

64

And I've loved you, I thought you loved me, you say you do."

"But it's not the same anymore. I don't want you -- the same way."

Tears coated her cheeks. She stared down at her nightie billowing over the small round of her stomach and the two calloused feet lined blue from bearing their children. She knew how she looked, her brown curls sticking out every which way, the corners of her eyes and mouth etched with fine lines, the gray strands at the temples. But they were married, they were growing old together. She thought he had loved her anyway, for herself.

"All right." She looked up. "Who is she?"

He choked. "It's Shawna Blake."

"As in, 'Hello, this is Medical Health Associates, Shawna speaking, how can I help you?' That Shawna? She has a last name?"

"Yup."

Alexander smiled weakly, and Meredith thought, how can you leave me for her when I'm so magnificent, when I'm funny even when you're gouging my heart out, I'll bet she can't make you laugh, this is temporary insanity, you can't leave me for that.

"Look, Alex. These things happen. I can't tell you I'm happy, but just because you've got the hots for your receptionist -- you're not a saint, nobody is."

She swallowed. This was torture. He had taken a knife and slashed her, and she would never be the same, but she would deal with those feelings later, alone. Right now, her job was to keep him here where he belonged, to keep her family together. There was more at stake than his guilt and her pain. They shouldn't do anything stupid.

"It's not just that, Meredith. I --."

He looked at her soulfully, pleading for help. Oh my God, she thought, and she put a hand to her head.

"I love her," he finished, almost sniveling. "I want to marry her."

"Okay, fine," said Meredith steadily, her chest clutching, but she stood there, firm. "Then get out."

She picked up his shirt and threw it at him and pointed to the bedroom door. He was still wearing his shoes. And he walked through the doorway, his tall frame warped by the weight of his sin. A minute later, the front door slammed, and the car in the driveway started up. She threw herself onto the rumpled bed and sobbed. And she imagined his stooped frame gradually straightening with relief and anticipation as he rushed into Shawna's arms.

"Mommy, I heard noises. Is Daddy home?"

Meredith looked up. Maggie stood in the doorway, her baby face rosy with sleep, her worn special blanket still knotted in one hand. Meredith grabbed hold of herself and held on tight.

"Say," Meredith asked, emerging from her reverie, "do you guys usually look through the wedding album with Shawna when you go to Daddy's house?"

Nobody responded. Maggie and Lucy both sat with their mouths slack and their eyes frozen, as Flora, Fauna, and Meriwether changed Sleeping Beauty's dress from pink to blue to pink to blue. Meredith punched the power button on the VCR remote, which immediately replaced the fairies with home shopping for fake gold chains. Her children blinked and stretched as if awakening from their own hundred year's sleep.

"So, Lucy, do you usually look at Shawna's wedding album when you go over there -- I mean, since we're talking about weddings and everything."

"Whose wedding?" asked Lucy.

"Sleeping Beauty's."

"Oh."

Lucy got up and shuffled into the kitchen. Meredith could hear the refrigerator door open and then the inner hum, as Lucy browsed for a snack. Meredith knew she should let this drop, it didn't matter, it didn't change anything, but she wanted to know.

"Do you guys look through the wedding album much?"

"Sometimes," said Maggie cautiously.

"Does it bother you at all?" Maybe it was bad for the children, and that was why she was asking. After all, Shawna was not known for her sensitivity.

"No." Maggie shrugged. "Why would it?"

"Well -- seeing Daddy marry somebody else."

"He did."

"Yeah. Um. Was it a nice wedding?"

"Why are you asking me this?"

"No reason. Just thinking about weddings, because of the movie, that's all. So, was it nice?"

"I don't know if you want to know this stuff."

"Well, I do," said Meredith. "I wouldn't ask you if I didn't."

"You never did before. Why didn't Daddy invite you, anyway?"

"You know, Maggie. It would have been awkward. Anyway, I wouldn't have wanted to come."

Liar, she thought. You longed to come. You have been holding yourself back from this picture for three years, but you wished you could have been there, to trip the beauteous Shawna, to snatch her veil and rip it off her bottle-blonde hair and shove it down her throat.

But, of course, she wouldn't have done that. She would have watched the princess push her sticky lips all over her husband's face, and she would have suffered. Which is why, in her vast maturity, she had attempted to stay as far away from the whole issue as possible. But it had been a long time, and now she wanted to know.

"Well, the wedding was nice. The cake was great, it had little pink icing roses on it, and in the middle was a real white lily. And they had these wedding mints, and they were white with different colored flowers on them made out of sugar." Maggie stopped. She had clearly completed the highlights.

"Did Shawna look pretty?"

"Yeah."

"She looked like a bride," said Lucy, wandering back in as she stuffed her cheeks with green grapes. One of the grapes squirted out and popped onto the coffee table, and Maggie and Lucy dissolved into helpless giggles.

I give up, thought Meredith. What was she doing? It didn't matter anyway. Because the story didn't end with the wedding, the way it did in fairytales. Four years had passed. That was certainly enough time for Shawna's charms to have faded and for Alexander to fall back under Meredith's original, more complicated spell. Now, if she could only find a spindle.

Chapter Six

Same Day

It was Friday night, and Suzanna was alone. She had been alone for several nights now, and they were terrible, awkward and frightening. But Friday night was worse, because it had once been so much more, because of her memories. Once, a million years ago, a car horn had honked, and she had run out to a Volkswagen packed with friends, wild with the freedom of no school for two whole days, and Friday night was extra, bonus time. When Chris and Catie were little, Bob would creep home after a long week's work, and they would go to a nice restaurant with linen and silver, just the two of them, and it was heaven, three hours alone, with waiters. Lately they had just stayed home and watched T.V., or played bridge with another couple, and sometimes Bob would work until 8:00 even on Friday night. But at least it was someone, sometime, an arrival to anticipate. Now Suzanna shifted aimlessly around the house, clicked the T.V. on and off, picked up a book and threw it down, checked and rechecked the doors to be sure they were all locked. The exhilarated young woman had melted away, leaving in her place a cold stub with nothing ahead but anxiety, tedium, and, if she were lucky, sleep.

She flicked on the kitchen lights. The marble floors and chrome appliances gleamed. She felt like a display mannequin in a model home gone haywire -- see the goofed-up lady in her perfect house, her face glowing white, her hands fluttering through her hair and aimlessly twisting together, not even Subzero can save her. Opening the refrigerator, she scanned the pathetic series of plates, a broiled chicken breast with a scoop of rice and two stalks of broccoli, linguini with marinara sauce and parmesan, a lamb chop with mashed potatoes and carrots, all neatly covered in cellophane, as if Bob might still walk through the front door and calmly request all the dinners that he had missed since he had left her on Tuesday. She slid out the linguini and examined it, the separating sauce with its ring of reddish fluid circling the base of congealed noodles. The plate swirled in a ghastly yellow light as the microwave hummed, and Suzanna drummed her fingers, watching the glow and wondering if the rays could penetrate the door and damage her. When the bell sounded, Suzanna removed the plate, pealed off the cellophane, and slid the steaming food into the garbage disposal. She repeated the process again and again, until, finally, she stood in the kitchen window with a neat stack of rinsed plates and the sound of dead bones grinding into dust.

She had changed from her work suit into a terry cloth robe. She wouldn't go out tonight, and there was no one for whom to look glamorous or even presentable. Except, perhaps, the man who was watching her. He saw her plainly, gaunt in the tightly drawn robe, her blonded hair sticking out carelessly on the sides, her aging face tight with loneliness. Would he find her despicable, she who had once flattered herself that she wore her years well, that she was petite and elegant and charming? Or would he, in his sickness, find her more appealing in her emptiness? Suzanna turned off the kitchen lights, and then she walked around the house shutting them all off, until she plopped down in the upstairs sitting room window, alone in the dark. Now she could see out, and no one could see in. She closed her eyes.

She must have dozed. A ringing sound woke her, and the clock said 9:15. The sound went again, the doorbell, someone was at the door. She slid into her slippers and groped toward the stairway, flicking on lights as she went. Who could be at the door at this hour? Suzanna pulled her robe closer and peered out the vertical window to the left of the double front doors. She couldn't see anyone, no car or truck or retreating form, until her eye caught the corner of a plain brown box tucked right up against the door, on the top step. She crossed to the right-side window and checked again -- still, no one was there, unless he was hiding in the hedge or had glued himself to the side of the house. Suzanna tried to remember the Boston Strangler -- how had he obtained entrance to women's houses, had he posed as the gas man, or had he simply left a package on the doorstep and then rushed in when they opened up? But, suddenly, she wanted the package more than anything. She was so tired and bored, it would be something to do, even for five minutes. Tentatively, she unlocked the door and eased it open. She glanced quickly around, snatched the package, and slammed the door shut.

Suzanna carried the box into the kitchen. It was taped tightly on all sides. She would need to slit it, but she didn't like the idea that the man outside -- if he existed, for, admittedly, no one had rushed in through the open door -- would see her with a knife in her hand. She reached into the drawer, but she held the knife low, and then she took the package to the table and turned her back to the window. Sliding the serrated edge across the heavy tape, she sawed the box open. Inside was a clear plastic bag containing a beige rubber glob and a pump. How wonderful, she had almost forgotten. Here was her salvation. The Inflatable Man had arrived.

Suzanna scanned the instruction sheet and then inserted the pump into the man's navel. Well, someone had a sense of humor, she thought, as she pushed air into him. Now he was her son, the protective son who stays home to care for his mother. Chris would get a chuckle out of this, though it might not be a good-natured one, more of a sneering, Mother-how-could-you-be-such-an idiot guffaw. Well, she had to do something for herself, it was perfectly clear that no one else would. The Inflatable Man was inexpensive, innocuous, and possibly effective, and at least he had brought some amusement to an otherwise miserable evening.

The man's legs and arms and neck soon filled into a sitting position, and he needed just a few more strokes to tighten his skin. Suzanna noted with some relief that he was not anatomically correct. If not molded into a sitting position, he would have stood about six feet tall, and he had a pleasant, slightly stupid face with a shade too much five o'clock shadow for her taste. She decided to smarten him up with a pair of old glasses, as in the advertisement, and then looked askance at his drawn-on hair. In the brochure he had been wearing a baseball cap, which would have been fine if she were going to take him for a ride, but seemed silly indoors.

Suzanna picked him up under her arm, well away from the window, carried him upstairs to her bedroom, set him on the floor, and pulled the shades. If he were to be her son, she should dress him in Chris's clothes, but Chris had taken everything he owned to Princeton. The easiest and most natural thing would be to dress the man as Bob. Suzanna had not told a soul that Bob had left her. If she dressed him up and propped him in the window, any passerby would assume he was her husband, relaxing at home after a hard day's work.

Suzanna smirked at the thought of putting the man in Bob's underwear, but sobered up when she saw that he had taken it all. Well, it didn't matter. After work, Bob always changed into casual clothes, a sport shirt and khaki slacks, and he had left most of those. She selected a bright plaid shirt that she had given Bob for Christmas and which he had worn only after she had specifically mentioned it, and a pair of old pants which probably would not fit his new, groovy lifestyle. Jamming the rubber limbs into the clothes proved difficult, the feet wanted to bend and get stuck, and the arms wanted to stay at his sides. She remembered dressing the infant Catie, thrusting her chubby arms into pink terry sleepers with bears on them. After several months, Catie had known what Suzanna wanted, she had helped, she was so smart.

Suzanna tucked in his shirt and zipped him up. The pants were a little short, but no one would see from outside. She found an old belt and a pair of glasses, and she put those on too. Really, he looked quite realistic, even without additional hair, and just as stiff as Bob. She could sit him in the window, right here in the sitting room. That way, if someone came over, she could show them in downstairs without having to scramble to shove him in the closet. And it was appropriate for the master to sit in his master bedroom suite, though truly, Bob never did. No matter. If he could leave her, he could certainly decide to sit somewhere else in the house. She set him in the wing chair under the reading light, right next to the window.

Now, what would he like to read? Bob didn't read much, the *Wall Street Journal* and an occasional spy novel. She ran downstairs and found the business section of the *Tribune*. He would have to be content with that. She switched on the reading light, opened the shades, gave the man an ostentatious kiss on the cheek, and stood back to admire the effect. He looked reasonably realistic even from here, and he certainly would from a distance. Occasionally she would change his clothes, at least until Bob came and took away the rest. Wouldn't Bob be surprised when he came in and found his replacement? Suzanna smiled, but she didn't really want that, she didn't want him to know how nervous she was. And she was feeling much better now, safer, almost confident. She picked up the phone and punched in Bob's office number.

"Hello, this is Robert Healey. Please leave a message after the tone."

"Bob, it's your wife, Suzanna. Remember me? Well, I wanted you to know that I'm doing fine without you, I knew you'd be terribly concerned. Also, I would appreciate it if you would give me advance warning before you come over to pick up your clothes. This is my house now, and I expect you to treat it as such. And,

I do hope, with all the secret planning you've been doing, that you've been saving your money. I'll be contacting a lawyer next week, and I'm sure that I'm entitled to a considerable sum after all these years, in addition to the house and the furniture. And you'll have to make a provision for Chris, of course. I don't know if you just expected me to roll over and die, but I won't, Bob, I won't be brushed aside as if I never existed. That's all. My lawyer will be in touch. Have a good day, and give my best to the floozy. Oh, Bob, you've turned out to be so disappointingly ordinary and squalid. I guess you never did have much imagination. I feel embarrassed for you."

Suzanna hung up. Well, that would certainly shake him up. If there were two things he was serious about, they were his checkbook and his facade. She didn't think she would really contact a lawyer, it seemed awfully soon, Bob still might change his mind. In the meantime, she had the Inflatable Man to protect her. She patted his arm gently so as to avoid bouncing him out of his chair, then went downstairs and rechecked the doors. In the morning she would call a locksmith, that would certainly get Bob's goat if he tried to come in unannounced. Her exhaustion finally overcoming her uneasiness, Suzanna climbed into bed, huddled on her side of it, and fell into a restless sleep.

Chapter Seven

Sunday, April 14, 1996

She came to him as he had known she would, as he had imagined so many times. Frank was invisible, he couldn't see himself, but he could see her floating towards him, her pale face framed in gold, her white limbs adrift in a cloud of chiffon, like a goddess. Suzanna reached out a hand, and he took it, he couldn't see himself, but he knew he had taken it, he felt its warmth and his own joy. He wanted her to come closer, on and on, until her gown flowed around him, her arms wrapping him like vines, and they fell gently back against the mist. But now he was in the half-light between waking and sleeping, because he knew the dream would change, and he longed to stay with Suzanna, but he was helpless, he could let the dream wash over him or he could wake up, those were his only choices. He sank back, and she was coming closer, her bare feet arched to meet him for a kiss. But before she could touch him, before their lips could brush or her soft breasts press against him, she began to change. Her blonde hair burned dark, and her expression curled in ridicule and disgust.

"No, Dinah, get out of here," he shrieked, as he clawed his way from sleep to the surface of his brown couch.

His skin felt greasy and slack, his mouth tasted sour, and, in a moment of disoriented fear, he could not think what time or even what day it was. The television grumbled as Frank sat up and scratched and checked his watch. It was five-fifteen on Sunday afternoon, and once again the AMC Family Classic had put him out. In a diaphanous gown, her hair fluffed around her regal cheekbones, Katharine Hepburn threw back her head and laughed. Frank reached for the remote control and punched her off.

Dinah had left him fifteen years ago, and he still couldn't get any peace. She had lied to him, laughed at him, trifled with his feelings, and now he couldn't get rid of her. He wanted to forget her, so that he could have Suzanna, but she just wouldn't leave him alone.

He had first seen her in the local Jewel, a metal mesh basket over her arm, a T.V. dinner and a can of soup, weekend provisions for one, just like his. She was tall and proud, her wavy dark hair setting off her angularity. Frank certainly didn't have the nerve to introduce himself, not even to make a passing remark or a dumb joke, just to get her attention. But a few weeks later he saw her again, and this time he followed her, ten feet behind, to the foot of a three-flat a few blocks west of his apartment. It was May, the weather was warming, the evenings dizzy with anticipation. After that, at night when he had nothing to do, he would stroll over and stand in front of her building, waiting for her to pass before the lighted window. He watched her from the street.

Until one day she caught him. She disappeared from the window, there was nothing unusual in that, and he waited, and in a few moments, she stepped up beside him.

"I can feel you watching me, you know. You trying to give me the creeps?"

"No, no," he said. "Sorry. I didn't mean to bother you. I'll leave."

She stood back, appraising him. "So, what is this -- you like me? Well, I guess if you were some rapist, you would have done it by now. Why don't you come up like a normal person, take a look from the other side?"

That was how it started. They walked around to the back and climbed the wooden stairs to the second floor landing, then in through the kitchen door. The apartment was small, but she had made it cozy, with curtains and throw pillows and flowered rugs. He was thirty-three, and Dinah was beautiful and warm, and he wanted her more than he had ever wanted anything in his life.

He took her out to dinner and to the movies on Saturday nights. He lived for the moment at the end, when she would kiss him in the kitchen, and he could feel her mouth soften, her body melting toward him, right before her red lacquered fingers pushed him gently out the door.

"Not til you make an honest woman of me," she would say, and she would laugh. "I don't come cheap."

So he would go downstairs and watch her. She knew he was there, she reveled in it, pulling off her stockings and her blouse and her skirt just inside the light. She would stroll past in a lacy bra and scant panties, lingeringly, as if she were promising him something. Then the light went out.

By August, Frank could hardly stand it any more. He didn't have much money, but one Saturday he went to the Jewelers' Building under the el tracks and bought a diamond ring in a velvet box. He pictured himself on bended knee, the open box outstretched, just like in an old movie. "Yes, yes," Dinah would murmur, the glow of love in her eyes, and the light would click off with him inside. He could hardly wait to see her, and he took the el back to her apartment and rang and rang the bell. When she didn't answer, he raced up the steps to the back door, but she had the place locked tight. So he went out to the sidewalk to wait. She wouldn't be gone long, he was only a half hour early for their date, and he had so much to tell her. He would just wait.

Frank waited for two hours. After a while, it got dark, and a light went on in Dinah's apartment. He rang the bell again and again, insistently; but no one answered. Then he saw a man, he was sure it was a man, it wasn't Dinah, walk past the window, and he bounded up the back stairs and pounded on the kitchen door until finally, the man opened it. He was wearing a v-necked undershirt, and the hairs on his chest coiled on the cotton like wires.

"What the hell's going on?" the man asked, as Frank pushed into the kitchen.

"Where's Dinah?" and then Frank heard footsteps clattering up the stairs. He would always remember that sound, her heels clicking towards him, filling him with hope and dread. She appeared in the doorway, breathless but composed.

"Oh, Frank, I forgot. This is Leo." She stared at Frank, standing silent and helpless, still clutching his box. "Is that for me? Sweet, but I hope you can get your money back. I enjoyed the meals and the movies -- you're a nice guy, Frank, you really are -- but you're too damned slow for me. Leo here is more my style."

Dinah's eyes met Leo's, and he grabbed her, pressing his body up against hers, their mouths meeting in a deep, moist kiss. Leo's hand reached under the back of her shirt, pulling her tight against him. Frank brushed by them and stumbled toward the stairs.

"And don't come back," Leo shouted after him. The last sound he heard was Dinah's pealing laughter.

Now Frank stood up and shuffled to the bathroom. The past was past, but it still had a way of seeping into the present and infecting things. The T.V. news spouted drivel about the healing process, sticking a stuffed bear at the site of a car wreck or murder, and then getting on with your life. But it wasn't that easy. Dinah had torn something inside him, and he knew, no matter how many years passed, he would never completely recover.

Frank checked the clock, five forty-five now, and he realized he was hungry. He padded into the kitchen and opened the refrigerator. Two beers, a few slices of Wonderbread, a jar of mustard, a slice of bologna, and some American cheese. It wasn't much, but it was enough for supper, probably better than most other bachelors did. He pulled everything out and dumped the bread onto the counter.

Suzanna was probably preparing dinner for Bob right now. Frank pictured her in stocking feet, moving lightly about the kitchen, grating fresh parmesan and slicing tomatoes, stirring a rich sauce on the stove and boiling water in a large copper pot. The whole house would smell warm and spicy. She would serve the food on flowered plates with crusty bread and wine, and she would sit across from him, twirling a noodle, her eyes bright and gentle. Frank loved her tininess, her delicate competence, like a fairy from a storybook.

He squeezed mustard onto a bread heel, and the doorbell rang. His heart jumped, he couldn't help it. He had been thinking so much of Suzanna -- was it possible that she had felt him pulling her closer, that she had come to him on her own? Maybe her husband had become more violent, and she had rushed to Frank for help. Or maybe she simply could not deny her emotions anymore, she wanted to be with him, he knew she was drawn to him, he knew it. And at the same time, he knew it was absurd, and he tried to calm down -- but absurd did happen, and he ran to the door and hopefully, lovingly, jerked it open.

Oh, it's you," he said, and his face fell, he was inhospitable and rude. "What are you doing here?"

Brenda loomed in the doorway, a full grocery bag only partially concealing her large gray head and matronly bust. She was his most loyal employee, and he depended on her. But she had no grace or charm, she was mercilessly efficient, and she was one of the homeliest women he had ever seen.

"I'm sorry," she said. "I know I should have called first, but I was passing by."

"Come in," Frank said dutifully, trying to remember himself. "What are you doing around here?"

"Well, I live nearby, about five blocks north, actually. I thought you knew that." Brenda seated herself primly on the couch, her knees together, the grocery bag on her straight navy skirt.

"No, I didn't. Can I take your bag?" What was this woman doing here, his employee, unannounced and now rooted to his couch on Sunday night? Barefoot and

81

disheveled, he did not feel comfortably authoritative as he did in the office, and he was painfully aware of his pitiful supper ingredients abandoned on the counter behind her.

"Actually, it's for you. I was picking up some groceries, and a few of the items I wanted were buy-one-get-one-free, you know how they do those promotions. Well, I couldn't use two, living alone as I do, but it seemed a pity to waste the opportunity, to let the store get the advantage." She deposited the grocery bag on the floor next to her and stood. "So, I guess I'll be going."

"All right. Thank you. That was awfully nice of you," Frank murmured, guilty that he was giving her the bum's rush, but too relieved to be friendly and risk her staying. "And now I know we're practically neighbors," he added. "I'm surprised I never noticed. You should have told me," he said stupidly.

Brenda faced him solemnly. "I'll see you tomorrow morning."

"Yes. It'll just be the three of us, like old times. Suzanna will be in Detroit for the day. Well, we'll have to struggle through without her," he smiled, opening the door.

"I'm sure we'll manage," Brenda said, and she walked out.

Frank closed the door and approached the grocery bag. One box of instant oatmeal, a plastic jug of Jewel brand syrup, a bag of onions, and a head of lettuce. An odd assortment, but the lettuce would be good on his sandwich. He lifted it from the bag and resumed his thoughts of Suzanna.

Rain was falling in angry slashes across the sky. Bob had planned to pick up a rotisserie chicken dinner from the dive around the block, but he could almost feel the wind whirling sheets of water past his tilted umbrella and soaking his jacket, his splashed cuffs clinging to his ankles. It wasn't worth braving the rain for a greasy drumstick in a styrofoam box. Listlessly, he turned from the window and crossed the empty living room to the kitchen. At least the kitchen, with its built-in cabinets and appliances, looked lived in. He opened the refrigerator, the white walls and chrome shelves glittering coldly, and reached for the quart of skim milk and loaf of whole grain bread, to keep him young and trim. If he had some butter, he could make toast, but he had forgotten to buy any, butter was one of the things he assumed they always had, a staple. But there was no they now, no flour or sugar or coffee, he would even have to buy salt. The wooden cupboard shelf felt gritty, Suzanna had always lined them with paper of some kind, he would have to look into it. He pulled out a napkin and a paper cup, lined up four slices of bread on the oven rack, and turned it on broil.

He thought of the Kenilworth house, all the things he had worked so hard for and yet taken for granted, plates and glasses and silverware, beds and towels and sheets and mattress pads, his stereo and the large T.V. and tables and chairs. Bob had planned to let Suzanna stay in the house, at least in the short term, until they could divide the property legally. But he hadn't realized what he was giving up. And, while he certainly hadn't imagined that Suzanna would be popping over with casseroles, he also hadn't thought that she would be vindictive, threatening to steal his hard-earned capital, and not even asking where he was living or offering him any of their numerous spare blankets. He had tried to be considerate, to wait until she could take care of herself before he left. They had been married twenty years, it wasn't nothing, he wasn't just going to dump her, and he had expected the same in return.

Damn, the toast was burning! Smoke oozed out of the oven, and he threw open the door and realized he had no hot pad, not even one of those checked towels Suzanna always left near the sink. He picked up the paper cup and wedged it under the rack and pulled, and the rack did slide out, but the wax on the cup melted and dripped onto the oven door. The top of his toast was black, while the bottom was still soft and disgustingly fibrous. Well, fine, he wasn't particularly hungry, and it would be good for him to lose a few pounds. He would eat again tomorrow at work, he would have lunch with Treena and remind himself why he was doing this.

Bob dumped the bread into a plastic bag and wandered into the bedroom. He didn't even have a bed, just a sleeping bag on top of an air mattress on top of the synthetic carpet covering a layer of cheap plywood. Chris's old portable television stood on the floor nearby. He supposed he ought to call one of those furniture rental companies, but it seemed a shame to pay through the nose for an acrylic dinette and a gray felt couch when he had much better quality items just a few miles away.

Bob sat on his sleeping bag and leaned against the wall. Who did Suzanna think she was, anyway, bossing him around, leaving him nasty messages and pretending she was entitled to everything he owned? He could see her, curled up like a cat in the family room he had built, cradling one of his ceramic mugs of fancy spiced tea, contentedly watching a premium cable channel on his large-screen color T.V. She had never worked a day in her life until a few months ago, and she had already received far more than she deserved for leading the life of a lady of leisure and poisoning his son against him and killing his daughter.

She had gone to the Jewel. The one thing he had asked her to do, watch the kids, in return for which she received a fancy house and designer clothes and a lavish allowance, and she couldn't even accomplish that. She had run to the store to pick up a few things for dinner and left a five-year-old under the supervision of an irresponsible teenager. Any fool could have predicted the outcome, and then to act as if she and Chris were blameless, as if he were the one with the problem because he loved his daughter. Well, he wasn't going to stand this any longer. He would drive to the house and take everything he could cram into the BMW, china and silver and blankets and linens, and then he would go back with a moving van and take all the large items he wanted, a bed for Christ's sake.

Although, Bob realized now, as he thought about it, it would really make a lot more sense for Suzanna to move out. Truly, Bob had always imagined Treena and their daughters in Kenilworth, Treena cooking in the country kitchen while she watched the girls play in the big backyard. Really, it was pointless for him to move his furniture out if all he was going to do was pay Suzanna some token for her portion of the house and then move back in himself. He needed a house, he had a growing family, but Suzanna could live anywhere, she was the one who was alone. Of course, getting her out of there might be tricky, even ugly, considering her current attitude. Moving out his furniture would be easier, since it only required brute force, he didn't need to convince her of anything. Still, if worse came to worse, brute force would work on Suzanna too. She was a lot smaller than the large screen T.V.

Standing in her apartment elevator, Brenda pushed the button for the fourth floor and waited. The machine buzzed disturbingly, bumped, and then rose, dragging open at her hallway, chipped doors punctuating dirty beige walls. Still, it would be a relief to be home, to step inside the familiar space and shut out the world. She had taken a risk, she had asked and received her answer, and now she couldn't even dream anymore.

She jiggled her key, and the doorknob turned, cold against her hand. Everything she owned was in this room, her books and her comfortable tweed chair, her wool cardigans in practical colors, and her smuggled cat Brando, her one act of defiance. Brando had curled himself onto the blanket she had left folded on the couch. He blinked when she entered and then sank back, reassured, to a purring doze.

Brenda closed the door and twisted the locks. This was not a good neighborhood. She had lived in a better one before, more trees, fewer thugs, but it was farther away from Frank. She had worked loyally for that man for ten years now, but only five years ago could she admit her feelings to herself, and only later could she imagine that somehow he might learn to love her back. Still, he went about his business, oblivious to the doughnuts she brought him, the special coffee and the clean desk and the attention she lavished on a job which barely paid her bills. She had continued to hope, and just to enjoy being near him -- until Suzanna Healey arrived. That Frank was smitten with Suzanna was immediately, sickeningly obvious. She was petite, rosy and white, with anxious blue eyes, expensive clothes, and trim ankles over tiny feet. She was Cinderella come to the ball, and it didn't even seem to matter to Frank that she was married.

Brenda walked into the kitchen and began to put away the groceries, the twins of the groceries she had brought Frank. It gave her some comfort to know that in the morning she and Frank would sit down to the same oatmeal, even thought they wouldn't sit down together. Oh, the idea of sitting with Frank at breakfast, of sharing cereal and washing his dish and brushing against him after sleeping in the same bed -- it made her almost dizzy with joy. But tonight she had finally taken a step, she had seen his home and his shoeless feet and his rumpled hair, and she knew beyond doubt that he did not want her. He didn't see her at all. All he could think about was Suzanna.

Brenda sat on the couch and quietly, miserably, stroked Brando's fur. He turned over, his nose in the air, permitting her to rub his stomach, graciously allowing her to love him. At least, before Suzanna, Frank had done the same. Suzanna should have stayed in her Kenilworth mansion with her bridge group and her garden club and whatever women do out there, she had so much, men just fell at her feet. With a snap of her fingers, Suzanna could have everything Brenda had worked for over the last ten years. Brenda sat up straight and clenched her fists. She could not allow that to happen.

Chapter Eight

Monday, April 15, 1996

Suzanna paid the cab driver and stepped out into the night.   April is the cruelest month, especially in Chicago, she thought, as the cold damp penetrated her trench coat and her sheer stockings. Pausing, she looked up at the house, a misplaced plantation, empty and haunted and gleaming.

In the second floor window, in the thin radiance of the reading lamp, sat her protector, the Inflatable Man. Suzanna was pleased to see how real he looked from the street, though unnaturally still, and his shirt appeared darker than she had remembered, a trick of memory or the light. Suzanna walked up the slate path to the double doors and fumbled the key into the lock. She had turned off the outdoor light when she left for Detroit this morning, and it was difficult to maneuver by the haze of the old-fashioned street lamp. She should have turned off the reading lamp and moved the Inflatable Man from the window as well, but she had forgotten in her rush to leave.

Suzanna picked up Monday's mail from the floor and quickly leafed through it, nothing but junk, and a tuition bill from Princeton, she would have to speak to

Bob about that. The answering machine was beeping, and as she kicked off her shoes and walked over to it, an image of the Inflatable Man, as she had just seen him, flashed, needling, into her head. Suzanna paused, crinkling her forehead, struggling to push through the prick of concern, until finally she realized he wasn't holding his newspaper. Well, it must have fallen. Or maybe he had put it aside because he had read all of the articles. She smiled slightly as she pushed the message button.

The first two calls were hang-ups. She hated that, a moment's silence and then a crackly, rummaging sound, and finally the dial tone of rejection. Suzanna was hoping for a message from Chris reporting he had enjoyed his spring break and had driven back to school safely and was preparing to buckle down for the last couple of months before he came home for the summer. It appalled her that he had been within a few miles of her for the last week, and she had seen him only that one horrid time, when he had fought with her and Bob. Unless he had talked to his father, which seemed unlikely, Chris didn't even know that Bob had moved out. There could be a message from Bob, she had never received a response to the voice mail she had left him on Friday, but she hadn't really expected one. After the third beep, a voice came on.

"Hello, Suzanna, it's Frank. It's about three p.m. I know you're not home yet -- it's just that I'm worried about you, and I think there are some important things we need to discuss. I just wanted to say that much, to prepare you, so that you can be thinking about it. I'll talk to you soon."

The machine beeped four times, signaling the end of the messages. Suzanna frowned. She thought that she had been doing well at work and that Frank liked her, so what was the problem? It was silly of him to worry her with a cryptic message so late in the evening. Maybe she would call him now, it would be better than twitching all night. Because she really wanted to keep this job. It wasn't the best job in the world, but with Catie and Chris and now Bob gone, it was all she had.

Suzanna picked up the phone, and then she put it down. She would wait a few minutes, until she was feeling less frazzled. She would go upstairs and clean herself up and change into her night clothes, and then she would come down and fix a cup of tea, and finally, when she was relaxed, she would call Frank back, apologize for the late hour, it would be about 9:45 by then, still within the realm of reasonableness, and ask him courteously what this was all about.

Suzanna began to climb the stairs. She had slipped her shoes back on so that she could hold her briefcase in her left hand and the banister with her right. Her feet clicking slowly against the oak, she realized how tired she was after travelling and meetings and worrying messages and now, confronting the house alone. Last Tuesday, when she first found out that Bob had left her, she was not sure she could cope at all, but now, after almost a week, she thought she would be able to sleep if she could just get the problem with Frank straightened out. She would adjust to Bob's absence as she had somehow integrated Catie's death into her life. Maybe someday it would even turn out to be a positive thing. Maybe she would find herself -- right now, she didn't even know if she were lost or not. She and Chris would get along better, Bob was the antagonist in that situation. She didn't know what was wrong with Bob. He was so proud of Chris, a son at Princeton.

Suzanna clattered onto the top step and walked the few feet to the door of the master bedroom suite. The sitting room door was closed. She didn't remember shutting it, she never did, why would she, and she backed up a step and wondered what to do. She was about to turn around, to run back downstairs and out the front door and just keep running the five blocks to the police station, when she realized she wasn't thinking clearly. Bob must have come for his clothes today, that would explain everything, the newspaper and the closed door and the funny nibble she had felt in the back of her mind ever since she had stepped out of the cab and faced the house.

Suzanna reached out, turned the knob, and pushed the door open. She took one step inside, and just as it occurred to her that Bob couldn't have come today after all, her mouth opened, and the pricks in her head sparked out through her arms and legs, and her stomach clutched. On the floor in front of her lay a clump of clothes trailing flattened rubber. Then the Inflatable Man stood up out of his chair and shot her dead.

Chapter Nine

Tuesday, April 16, 1996

"I'd really love to drive a new Mercedes, if only I could afford one."

"Well, chances are you can afford one, you just have to know where to shop."

"But I'm unhappy going from dealership to dealership, being talked down to and pressured."

Meredith groped for the station button on the car radio and punched it. She despised that commercial, materialistic whiner meets sleazy product consultant, the American dream at its worst. And, after stuffing Maggie and Lucy with Fruit Loops and dragging them to school on her way to d-u-l spells work, she didn't need any more aggravation, especially from someone whose life was incomplete without a hunk of metal that cost as much as Meredith's house.

"The patter of footsteps across the hand-woven mats covering the mud floor in Kiawa's twig hut ..."

Ah, public radio. Meredith's brain calmed to the drone of news from countries no one had ever heard of. It was Tuesday morning, an ordinary, non-news day for Ms. Bennett, prosecutor of shoplifters, vandals, and the odd felon. Later she was due in good old Courtroom F for her regular mish-mash of petty crooks and no-shows. After seventeen years, she could do this part of her job in her sleep.

Turning west onto Old Orchard Road for her final descent into the North Suburban Courthouse parking garage, she punched the station button again for actual news, the latest fires and molestation in jurisdictions several miles distant and a world apart from the North Shore.

" ... the woman's body was found in her bedroom in Kenilworth early this morning. She appeared to have been shot once in the chest. Robbery did not appear to be a motive, and the police have no suspects at this time. This is the first apparent homicide in the prosperous suburb in fifteen years."

A murder in Kenilworth, her old neighborhood. Meredith reached for her newly acquired car phone, her doff-of-the-cap to modern technology. Although tiny by Chicagoland standards, several thousand people did live in Kenilworth, and the victim was unlikely to be anyone she knew. She felt a flash of guilt -- could the dead woman be the lovely Shawna? No, that wasn't even funny.

"Kenilworth Police."

"Hello, is Detective Reed there? This is Meredith Bennett calling, from the State's Attorney's office."

Meredith turned into the drive leading up to the courthouse.

"Detective Reed here."

"Hi, Al, it's Meredith Bennett. I understand you have a homicide. Any identification?"

"Hello, Meredith.   Yes, her name's Suzanna Healey, 287 Oxford."

"Oh my God."

Meredith's legs started to shake. She shouldn't be upset, Suzanna was only an old neighbor, Meredith was a professional, she'd dealt with murders before, well, a couple, anyway. But her body quivered all on its own. She pulled into a parking space and sat, to catch her breath.

"You okay, Meredith -- did you know her?"

"Yes, sorry, I'm okay." She paused. "Al -- I'll be right over."

"All right. I'm heading over to the residence. I'll see you there."

Distractedly, she backed into the flow of incoming employees and wound down to the street.

Meredith slowed the Honda to round the tight curve in front of Suzanna's house. Years ago, when she and Alexander had decided on the Tudor a few doors down from the Healeys' white Colonial, they had particularly liked Kenilworth's country lane feel, stone bridges spanning a dribbling creek, even an occasional hill, so unusual for Chicago. But while a teenager tearing home from high school might have been able to manage on a typical Chicago grid, one could not always maneuver Oxford's tight turn. Six years ago, a New Trier junior had missed this curve completely, ripping across the parkway grass and into little Catie Healey, quietly chalking daisies on the sidewalk only a few yards

95

from her front door. It didn't bear thinking about, it was over and done. But how did you deal with such a grief? And now her mother was dead, murdered. It was too much for one family to bear.

Meredith picked her way past several police cars and walked up the path to the familiar black double doors. She had stood here with a casserole dish of beef burgundy and an applesauce cake, pointless offerings to a family too heartsick to eat. But they had to know that people cared, friends and neighbors who didn't know what to say or how to help, but who wanted to do something. Meredith had added her cake to the stack on the kitchen counter and shoved the dish into the laden refrigerator, filled with unfamiliar, perplexing containers. Poor Chris, just a boy then, must be back at Princeton now. Meredith wondered if he had been told, he would want to come back here to be with his father. A mother and a father and a child, they were a family. So were a mother and her two daughters, she hoped. But was an aging father and his almost grown son? Meredith wondered if they would make the effort, if they would even know how to begin.

A uniformed policeman answered the door.

"Hello, I'm Meredith Bennett, from the State's Attorneys office. Detective Reed is expecting me."

The officer ushered her into the front hall. The sight of the yellow police tape across the familiar stairway caught her unexpectedly. Everything was still here -- to the right, the cherry dining room table displaying pewter candlesticks and a Waterford bowl, to the left, the family fireplace, with photographs of Chris as a high school hero, of a young Suzanna in pooling white satin, and peeking from behind, a small, silver framed Catie, forever grinning toothlessly before her last five birthday candles. The color scheme was muted, pink and beige -- Suzanna would never have tolerated the gaudy yellow strip dangling between the banisters. Meredith reached out for the wall, and the officer grabbed her arm.

"Are you all right, Ma'am?"

"Yes, fine, just give me a moment." She lowered her head, took a deep breath, and raised it. "Is Detective Reed here?"

"Yes, this way, when you're ready."

The officer led Meredith under another police tape into the kitchen. Al Reed was standing in the mudroom with an evidence technician, examining the back door.

"Ah, hello, Meredith. Signs of forced entry. The perpetrator must have smashed the window pane and reached through and unlocked the door. We haven't got any clear prints yet, the knob's smeared. But, this suggests that the perp was not a family member."

His matter-of-fact professionalism bolstered her, but she still leaned on the counter for safety. "Right. Unless he forgot his key, or decided not to use it to divert suspicion from himself. What's with the guns?"

"Someone in the house is a collector. There's a locked cabinet upstairs containing some antique pistols, but we found these two in the rack down here."

"Is one of them the murder weapon?"

"I don't think so, they look clean, and the guns upstairs are locked up tight. Of course we'll check them all out, and we're conducting a search of the premises."

"They must belong to the husband, Bob Healey. I can't believe Suzanna would be interested. I used to live a few doors down, so I know the family a little. They didn't keep guns in the mudroom in my day, but that was several years ago, when the kids were around."

"Do you think they could be involved, the husband or the son?"

"I don't know. I knew the son a little, enough to say he seemed like a nice boy, but it's been a long time, and the husband was usually at work. And as long as people mow their lawns and don't play their music too loudly, the neighbors always think they're model citizens. Who found her?"

"The son. He's in the den now, resting on the couch. He said he came over to say goodbye before he drove back to Princeton after spring break."

Meredith frowned. "On Tuesday morning? And why wasn't he staying here to begin with?"

"He hasn't been very communicative, and I didn't want to push, not yet, anyway. Maybe you could talk to him. He might be more open with an old family friend."

"I'd be glad to. Is his father in there too?"

"No. That part's a little strange. Chris says he came by early, about six a.m. He certainly expected to see his father at that time of day, but there was no sign of him. We couldn't locate him until about nine, when we reached him at his office. He's on his way."

"I'd like to talk with him too. First --" Meredith hesitated, she did not want to do this, but she knew it would help her understand "-- would you take me upstairs?"

"If you're sure you're up to it. It's not a pretty sight."

They walked into the hallway. Detective Reed unhitched the yellow tape, and they both began to climb.

"Turn right at the top."

Meredith had not been upstairs since the dark days immediately after Catie's death, when she had gone up during the post-funeral gathering to use the bathroom. The second room on the right had been Catie's, and the door had been half open. The pink and white ruffled curtains had grabbed her, and the heap of stuffed animals, and the small sneakers aligned neatly beside the bed. Now Meredith could see a sliding door, and cold tile. She turned right, gripped and stared.

Suzanna was still there. She was lying in a face-down bunch almost at Meredith's feet, as if, even in death, she had tried to arrange herself with a minimum of fuss. Her arms were folded beneath her, her hands attempting to cover the hole in her chest. Despite her efforts, a flared red stain on the cream rug surrounded her shoulders like poppy petals. A few feet away sprawled a heap of men's clothing, a plaid shirt and belted pants, like a second, bodiless victim.

"Apparently, she died from a single bullet wound to the chest." Al Reed touched her arm lightly. "I'm sorry, I know this must be hard for you. They'll be taking her away shortly. That pile of clothes over there is a little bizarre, and we're going to keep that detail from the media."

"What is it?"

"It appears to be an inflatable man."

Meredith turned to Al.

"I don't know what they had it for. It was a life-size rubber man that you inflate with a bicycle pump. It was new, just a few days old. The box was in her closet."

"So -- is it dead?"

99

Al smirked. "Yup, it's dead all right. Shot also."

"Weird." And with that succinct ineptitude, Meredith burst into tears.

Al put his arm around her and led her back down the stairs. "We'd be glad to have your help, but are you sure you can handle this?"

"Sorry. Yes. I'm sure. Talk to me. Tell me more -- anybody see anything?"

"Not much, so far. We talked to a neighbor who noticed a man sitting in the upstairs window the last couple nights. She thought it was a little unusual, but she didn't stop and study him, she just noticed. It could have been the inflatable guy, or it could have been the husband."

"What did you tell him on the phone?"

"Not much -- that his wife was dead. He asked were we sure and what happened. I told him she'd been shot in the upstairs sitting room, probably sometime last night. He sounded like he was choking, and then he was quiet for a minute, and then he said he'd be right over."

The doorknob turned, and Bob Healey opened the front door and stepped into the hallway. He was wearing a gray suit, a starched white shirt, and a strained facial expression. He deposited two leather-trimmed suitcases neatly beside the stairs, just beneath the trailing yellow police tape.

"Bob, hello," Meredith said, stepping forward and brushing his arm. "I'm so sorry."

"Um -- thank you."

He looked confused, and Meredith realized that he could remember her only vaguely as a neighborhood mom, her face floating above an unwanted casserole.

100

"I'm Meredith Bennett, I'm an Assistant State's Attorney helping with the investigation. This is Detective Reed from the Kenilworth Police Department. Let's go into the living room and sit down. I'm sure this must be a terrible shock for you."

Meredith looked up at Al Reed, who nodded and turned back toward the kitchen. She led Bob into his own elegant living room and sat on a stiff chair. Bob picked the couch opposite, the farthest spot from Meredith in the seating group. Meredith was surprised at his silence, his lack of curiosity and ability to maintain control in the face of his wife's sudden death.

"I'd like to ask you a few questions, if you're up to it," she said.

"Go on."

"When was the last time you spoke to Suzanna?"

"That would be --" he hesitated "-- last Monday."

"You mean a week ago, on, let's see, April 8?"

"Yes. As I said."

"Were you away on business?"

"No, I was here in Chicago." Bob looked irritated. "We had separated."

"I see," Meredith said, but she did not see. When she had run into Suzanna in the supermarket ten days ago, Suzanna had given not the slightest hint that her marriage was in trouble. Certainly, the middle of the Jewel food store might not be the best place to bare your soul, and particularly not to Meredith, whom she hadn't seen in a couple of years. Still, a marriage on the brink of destruction might have a way of barreling through one's reserve. Unless Suzanna did not know herself. This, as Meredith well knew, was possible, under circumstances of which she was also well aware.

101

"What did you discuss last Monday?"

"Look, I don't know, the weather, the usual things."

"So you didn't tell her then that you were moving out? Why don't you just tell me how this went."

"Frankly, I don't see what business it is of yours."

Meredith just looked at him. Bob flushed and then leaned forward, rubbing his forehead.

"All right then, but this isn't easy. You've got to understand, I can barely think, don't hold me to the letter of any of this. Monday was a normal day. We both went to work, came home, had dinner, went to bed."

"That's here, in this house?"

"Yes, of course. The next day, last Tuesday, Suzanna went to Detroit on business. She has a good job now, you know, she really doesn't need me for much anymore. Didn't. Oh, God, I don't know." He put his head down, and his shoulders trembled. Meredith waited. When Bob looked up, his eyes were red, and he wiped his nose with the side of his hand. "After she left, I packed some clothes, and I dropped them off at my new apartment in Chicago. I'd rented it a few days before. Then I continued downtown to work. I left her a message explaining that I had moved out and that I would pick up the rest of my things later."

"And you never heard from Suzanna again?"

Bob looked away, his features sagging, as if he had melted. "No. I never did."

"She got the message on the answering machine that you were leaving her after -- what twenty years -- and she just let it drop?"

"Well, wait. We never spoke again, but she did leave me a message at work, nothing hysterical, just a goodbye and good luck. What did you expect her to do, hurl herself in front of my car? It wasn't like that between us, our relationship was dead. That's why I left."

"So, what's with the suitcases now?" Meredith indicated the front hall with her head.

"I might as well move back in. This is my house, and it's a lot more comfortable than the apartment."

Meredith stared at him. "You want to move right back in, to the house where your wife was murdered a few hours ago. I don't even know if that's possible yet. This is a crime scene." In case you hadn't noticed, she thought.

"Look, Meredith. I'm as shocked and horrified by Suzanna's death as anyone, certainly more than you are. But she's gone, and there's nothing I can do about it. I was passing the apartment on my way out here from the office, and I stopped for a moment to grab my suitcases, which I still hadn't unpacked. This is my home. It makes perfect practical sense."

"You'd been there a week and you hadn't unpacked."

"That's right. If you think that's unusual, you don't get out much."

Actually, she didn't find it unusual. Alexander was the same way, and she was certain her daughter Lucy would live out of a suitcase for four years of college unless her roommate dumped her clothes into a drawer. Meredith stopped for a moment and studied the grieving husband. He seemed in some ways shaken, and he claimed to be distressed. Yet, in other ways, he was chillingly composed.

"Bob, where were you last night, starting from about six o'clock?"

He looked at her steadily. "At six, I was still at work. I left at around 6:30, and I went home."

"To the apartment? What's the address?"

"It's 1829 North Cleveland. I made myself some dinner, I watched the Bulls game, and I went to bed."

"Did you have any contact with anyone after 6:30 -- did the doorman see you come in, do you have a parking lot attendant, any phone calls, did you go out again?"

"I don't have a doorman or a parking lot attendant, it's just a three-flat, and I didn't go out again. As for calls, let's see. I called the office for messages before I ate, at around 7:30. While I was eating, I got a hang-up call, it was probably around a quarter to eight. I have no idea who it was, probably just a wrong number. And that was it."

"Meredith?"

Al Reed was standing in the doorway, and next to him, head hanging, slumped Chris Healey. Bob turned chalk white and stood up.

"Chris, I thought you were back at Princeton. What are you -- ?" And he stopped.

"No, Dad, I'm right here. Just like you," Chris said. His cheeks reddened, and he put his hands over his eyes.

Bob took a step toward him. "Son…".

Chris shook his head and raised a finger to warn his father away.

"Meredith," said Al, "we're going to take Chris back to his friend's dorm room, where he's been staying. He's tired, and he wants to rest there for a while."

104

"You can stay here with me, Son," Bob said, stepping forward.

Chris flinched, as if his father had slapped him. "Stay away from me," he said.

"Okay." Meredith moved over to Chris and touched his shoulder. "Give Detective Reed the address, and I'll come see you later. Is there somebody there to take care of you?"

Chris nodded and rubbed his eyes, like a little boy.

"I'm so sorry, Chris," she said.

"Oh, Mr. Healey," Al said, "I was wondering if you could come back with me for a minute." He gestured toward the kitchen, and they all followed. An evidence technician in the mudroom stepped aside. "Are these your guns?"

"Yes, I collect them. These two are British dueling pistols, Richard Wogden, from about 1830. I have more guns, of various types, upstairs, in a locked case."

"Did you only keep the two down here?"

"No, actually, there were three. The 1860 Colt revolver appears to be missing."

"These two are loaded. Would the revolver have been loaded also?"

"Yes. I -- cleaned and loaded them before I left last week. The pistols are very valuable, and they should be locked up, but I wanted Suzanna to be able to protect herself. She doesn't shoot, and dueling pistols are lightweight and easy to aim. These Wogdens have a hair trigger mechanism and are especially accurate. The revolver, of course, has the advantage of being able to fire several times without reloading. You don't mean somebody used it --." Bob frowned.

"We don't know anything yet, Mr. Healey. I just wanted to check that out with you."

Chris turned to Meredith. "What does he mean, before he left last week?"

Gently, Meredith placed her hand on Chris's back. "Your father left your mother last Tuesday. He moved into his own apartment temporarily. Now he wants to move back here."

"I -- I can't take anymore -- I've got to get out of this house," Chris said, rushing toward the front door. In the doorway he paused and turned back to his father. "Don't think you're going to get away with this, you subhuman piece of shit."

Chapter Ten

Same Day

Meredith drove west into the odd mesh of highways and fields and even a few cows only ten minutes beyond Winnetka's tennis courts. Turning north on Shermer just past the air strip, she eventually spotted number 621, a gray three-story shoe box displaying a billboard advertising available office space. Apparently Power Health Corporation, where Suzanna Healey had worked for the last months of her life, did not waste its money on crystal chandeliers.

After parking her Honda in the pitted parking lot, Meredith took the elevator to the second floor, an uninviting fluorescently lit hallway lined with closed doors. Entering Suite B-8, she found herself in a serviceable room containing three metal desks, a stack of cardboard boxes, and a file cabinet crowned with a Mr. Coffee machine and a cylinder of coffee whitener. At the front and back desks, two women talked on the telephone. The middle desk was unoccupied, though a neat stack of papers, a computer, a telephone, and a stapler indicated that it also had its mistress. Through a glass divider in the rear of the office, Meredith could see the lone man, the king of Power Health, in his inner sanctum. Although his desk was wood and his chair large and comfortable, in keeping with his elevated position, he was talking on the telephone too.

Meredith stood politely, waiting for the astoundingly retro woman at the front desk to complete her call and look up. While her beehive nodded and her crimson lips spat statistics, she clicked fake blue fingernails with fireworks erupting at their tips. In contrast, the woman at the back desk looked like a prison matron, with iron gray hair and a brown wool cardigan buttoned over a pigeonlike bust. Meredith could not imagine petite Suzanna, with her pink pearl fingernails and expensive pastel suits, confiding in either one of them.

"May I help you?" The beehive deposited the receiver and glanced up efficiently.

"Yes. My name is Meredith Bennett, and I'm from the State's Attorneys office. Is this where Suzanna Healey -- works?"

"Yeah." The beehive shifted forward in her seat and indicated the middle desk with a slight tilt of her head. "She didn't come in today, and she didn't call either. Is she okay? Cause, I mean, it's not like her, she's usually so responsible. Frank, that's the boss, he thought maybe she needed to sleep in after her trip yesterday." She leaned forward confidentially. "I'd like to see him show us that sort of consideration, but I guess we're not as important as Suzanna, are we?"

"Do you think I could talk to Frank for a minute?"

"Sure." She shrugged. "I'll see if he's free."

Rising from her desk, she wriggled to the back office, her tight, size fourteen skirt ticking like a pendulum above weakening scuffed red pumps. After a brief conversation, she stepped out, gesturing Meredith forward.

"Come on back, Hon."

As the prison matron glared and the beehive resumed her duties, Meredith picked her way back to Frank's office. She entered and closed the door.

"Hello. I'm Meredith Bennett, from the State's Attorneys office."

Frank stood weakly and then dropped down again. "Frank Nelson, Power Health. What can I do for you?"

He was a haggard, squinting man of about fifty, with receding gray hair, a paunch rolling over his brown belt and trousers, and a tired edge to his voice.

"I'm here about Suzanna Healey. She works for you, doesn't she?"

"Yes. Actually, I was beginning to worry about her, she's usually here by now."

"I would think so, it must be after eleven. You didn't call her house?"

"No. I thought she might need some extra sleep. She was on a business trip yesterday and got home late."

"Did you talk to her last night?"

"No. Of course, we all know her work schedule."

A thin film of sweat greased Frank's upper lip. On top of his desk, his meaty hands gripped each other, fingernails bitten to the nub.

"I'm afraid I have some shocking news. There's no easy way to say this. Mrs. Healey is dead."

Frank blanched, his lips pursed, and his arms clutched his stomach as if he were going to be sick.

"I'm so sorry, Mr. Nelson. Can I get you something?"

"No, no," he murmured, his eyes welling up. "I'm sorry. She was a -- fine employee."

"You must have been fond of her."

"Yes, well, that is -- we worked together a lot, and she was a big help to me, and I guess I took an interest in her, I guess I did."

"You liked her."

"Yes. Look, could you give me a minute?"

"Certainly."

Frank swiveled in his chair, so that his back was to Meredith. He bent over, his shoulders heaving, his breath coming in short, flat gasps. Meredith waited uncertainly for a moment and then rose from her chair and went to him. Glancing up, she could see the beehive tapping at her keyboard, while the matron stared shamelessly through the glass divider at the scene behind her.

"Frank, I'm so sorry," Meredith said, tentatively rubbing his back as if he were a stray dog.

He looked up, his homely, puffed face wet with misery.

"What happened?"

"She died in her home last night. She appears to have been shot."

"Shot," he sniffed, swiveling back around. "Who would want to -- do that?"

Meredith resumed her seat. "That's what we're trying to find out. We're trying to learn as much as we can about Suzanna's daily life. She must have spent a lot of time here."

"Well -- not a lot. She'd only been working here for about six months."

"But in such a small office, I'm sure she was a valuable employee."

"We don't usually get people like Suzanna. She's smart, she learns fast, and she presents herself well, she creates a good image for the company. Created."

"What did the other employees think of her? They must have been jealous, she'd been here such a short time, and you were giving her so much responsibility."

Frank looked confused. "I don't know. I never thought about it. Suzanna was special, different, she deserved special treatment. Anybody could see that."

"Did she have a friendly relationship with anyone in the office besides you?"

"Well, she was a pleasant person, but I don't think it went any farther than that. I can't imagine she saw the other girls after hours, if that's what you mean."

"And what about you -- did you see her after hours?"

"No, of course not. She -- was married."

"Are you married also, Mr. Nelson?"

"No, I'm not."

"Did you know that Suzanna and her husband had separated recently?"

"What? No, I didn't know that, she never told me, she never mentioned it. When did that happen?"

"About a week ago."

"No. She never told me anything at all."

Abruptly, Frank stood up.

"Just a couple more quick questions. First, just to be complete, strictly routine -- where were you last night after six o'clock?"

"I was at home in my apartment in Chicago."

"Do you live alone?"

"Yes."

"Did you go out at all, did you talk to anyone on the phone?"

"No, no. Look, I don't mean to rush you, Ms. Bennett, but I have a business to run here. And I need to -- tell the girls."

"I understand, thank you for your patience. If I could just get a list of the names, addresses, and phone numbers of everyone in this office and take a quick look through Suzanna's desk, I'll get out of your way for now."

"That's fine. I'll have Brenda write down the information for you, and I'll bring them both in here with me for a minute."

Meredith went back into the main office, as Frank indicated the middle desk, summoned his employees, and shut the door. She shuffled through Suzanna's neat files and tidy drawers, but she saw nothing personal except the small photo of Chris and Catie in a gold frame beside the computer. After a few minutes, the prison matron wordlessly deposited the address list on Suzanna's desk and then turned to rejoin Frank. When she looked through the glass divider to wave good-bye, Meredith saw the beehive gesticulating, while the matron, Brenda apparently, stood protectively beside him and stared stonily out at Meredith.

112

Shooting down the express lanes of the Kennedy, sloping concrete barriers enclosing a two-lane strip, Meredith felt like a marble blown through a tube in a dizzying arcade game. She stayed in the right lane, where she could sense her boundaries, and tried not to think about what would happen if she deviated a few inches to either side. Driving always had an air of unreality for her, a denial of the terrifying ease with which Maggie and Lucy could be rendered motherless. She exited at Ohio and made her way southeast on the grid of one-way streets to Chicago National Bank's massive building in the cavernous financial district. She asked for Robert Healey's office at the information booth and was directed to a bank of elevators a discreet distance from the public. On the third floor, Meredith settled into a leather-strap chair with a prop copy of the *Wall Street Journal* and a vacant expression until Bob's secretary came to greet her.

"Hi, I'm Natalie. So, we're all awfully upset about Mr. Healey's poor wife," Natalie asserted in a stage whisper as she escorted Meredith down the corridor. "So, I mean, what's going on -- was she really murdered? Why are you here -- I mean, no offense, but you don't suspect Mr. Healey do you, I mean, that's ridiculous."

"We're just trying to understand the Healeys' lives a little better. It's strictly routine. Is there somewhere private you and I could talk?" Meredith asked, as Natalie hovered next to her desk in the hall.

"Well, I suppose we could go into Mr. Healey's office. He said he wasn't coming back in today."

113

Natalie led Meredith into a large office with two windows, a couch, and a table displaying a telephone with an impressive array of buttons and a browning philodendron. She perched expectantly on the couch. Meredith shut the door and slid into the opposite corner.

"So, how did you hear about Mrs. Healey?"

"Well, Mr. Healey had to leave almost as soon as he got here, and he looked pretty upset, so I asked him was anything the matter. And he said that he might as well tell me, his wife had been shot, and I couldn't believe it, and neither could any of the other girls. So, Candice, she's two desks down, she has a radio, and we listened all morning, and we figured that the woman in Kenilworth, that was her. It's just awful. I talked to her on the phone sometimes, you know, Mrs. Healey, when she would call to talk to her husband, and she seemed like a very nice lady, polite, you know. He was usually busy, at a meeting or on the phone, and, 'Just tell him I called when you get a chance,' she'd say, no pressure or anything."

"Did Mrs. Healey ever come over here to the bank?"

"No, well, I only saw her once, a couple years ago, when they were going out to dinner with some clients. She was friendly, and pretty too, I remember. Poor thing, so many tragedies. First her daughter, and now this. It just goes to show."

"Goes to show what?"

"Well, I guess that living in a big, fancy house and wearing nice clothes isn't everything."

"Yes, well. Who are Mr. Healey's friends here? Who does he eat lunch with, for example?"

"Well, there's Mr. Katz down the hall, and Mr. Blake, and of course Treena Snider." Natalie pursed her lips in what Meredith assumed was discreet disapproval.

"Who's Treena Snider?"

"She's a junior vice president."

"And she and Mr. Healey were friends?"

"Some might call it that."

"What do you mean -- were they having an affair?"

"I honestly don't know," said Natalie with unusual care. "Mr. Healey doesn't seem like the type, I mean, he's never tried anything with me or anything. But, Treena Snider is very, you know, flirty, and Mr. Healey is still a man, even if he is old. Some women will do anything to get ahead, it's a little disgusting, between you and me. All I really know for sure is they ate lunch together a lot. But look at this."

Natalie leaped up, stepped over to Bob's desk, and grabbed a gold picture frame. Dramatically, she turned the photograph to face Meredith. Two small blonde girls in ruffled pink dresses smiled demurely from under matching spring bonnets. The older one bore a superficial resemblance to Catie Healey, Bob's dead daughter.

"Who are they?"

"They're Treena Snider's kids. I asked him, and he told me. They just appeared here a couple weeks ago. I mean, he's keeping a picture of Treena's children on his desk. Don't you think that's weird?"

In fact, Meredith thought it was very weird. "Is Treena Snider here today?"

"She certainly is," said Natalie. "Would you like to speak to her? I'll get her right now."

115

Soon Meredith heard the jingling of gold bracelets heralding Treena's approach. Meredith already knew, of course, that Bob had left his wife last week. And in her own unfortunate experience, men took this decisive step only after the replacement was conveniently in position.

"Hello -- oh my goodness. Where did this come from?"

Treena Snider, a lavish blonde of about twenty-eight, in a lime green suit and high heels which pushed her butt almost up to her ears, stuck out her hand for a shake and received instead the framed portrait of her daughters.

"It was on Bob Healey's desk. Thank you Natalie. You can shut the door on your way out." Natalie blinked disappointedly and backed out of the room. "Please sit down, Ms. Snider. I'm sure Natalie has told you the pertinent information. I'm sorry to be abrupt, but I'd like to get right to the point. Were you and Bob Healey lovers?"

Treena looked Meredith directly in the eye. "Certainly not. I am a happily married woman," she said primly.

"Why did you give him a photograph of your children?"

"I didn't. He must have taken it from my office."

"Were you aware that Bob Healey's feelings for -- your family -- were more than professional?"

Treena folded her long, white fingers. Her bracelets clinked softly.

"Yes, I was."

"Could you elaborate?"

116

It all came out in a rush. "Last week we were having lunch. It was an ordinary lunch in the cafeteria, nothing special, we had lunch together probably twice a week. And all of a sudden, out of nowhere, Bob told me he loved me and he wanted to marry me. I couldn't believe it. I mean, it's a little late, isn't it? I'm already married, with two kids, and so is -- was - he. Oh my God, you don't think --?"

Meredith ignored the question. "Is that what you told Bob when he declared himself to you -- that it was too late, you were both married?"

"No -- I -- I don't know what I said, he told me not to say anything, just to think about it. What could I say? He's an important man here at the bank. I didn't want him to turn on me. I didn't know what to do. I guess I just hoped it would go away, that he would, I don't know, realize it was a temporary testosterone rush and forget the whole thing."

"Did he tell you he left his wife last week?"

"Oh -- no. No, he didn't mention that. Well, actually, I haven't been alone with him since he -- proposed. I've been trying to avoid him, but nicely, you know. I don't want to hurt his feelings. But my husband was pretty upset about it. He's an artist, and they can be so emotional."

"You told your husband?"

"Yes, of course. Wouldn't you?"

Meredith supposed she would, if she still had one. It would have been kind of a kick, an ego builder, to make Alexander jealous for a change. Though it probably wasn't a change for Treena, from the look of her, and it certainly didn't seem to be an innocuous romantic game to Bob Healey.

117

"How did he react?"

"He -- his name is Craig -- he was angry, but, um, forgiving."

"Angry at you or at Bob?"

"Both of us, I guess. Look, where is this going? Because we didn't even know Suzanna Healey, except to smile hello to at cocktail parties, and she seemed like a very nice lady."

Meredith nodded. "Thank you for your time, Ms. Snider, and I'll be in touch if I have any more questions."

Treena stood up. "Can I have my picture back?"

"Let's leave it here for now, if you don't mind. I don't want Bob to think I took any of his things."

Treena frowned. "Okay," she said, and she left.

I give that picture five minutes after I'm gone, Meredith thought, and it's safe in Treena's briefcase. Meredith would have done the same thing herself.

Chapter Eleven

Same Day

"**S**o, since Alex will be working late, I was, like, wondering if I could take the kids out for dinner tomorrow night. And you too, if you're free. You are free, aren't you?"

Meredith was tired. After her expedition to Northbrook and then downtown, she had skipped visiting Chris in Evanston to pick up her own kids from After School Fun. Now Shawna sounded jittery, and talking to her about anything, let alone dealing with the prospect of breaking bread with her, was too much to cope with.

"That's really very nice of you Shawna, but it's a school night."

"Oh, I know, I know. I just thought the California Pizza Kitchen or something, just someplace quick like that."

"The California Pizza Kitchen?" Meredith glanced up to see Maggie's head bobbing maniacally, like a toy dog with a spring neck shifting on the dashboard on a bumpy road. Exhibiting a similar inclination, Lucy was making disgusting slurpy sounds, running her tongue around the outside of her mouth and rubbing her stomach in an imagined orgy of gluttony.

"Okay, fine, they'd love to. It's nice of you to think of them."

She sounded like such a prig. Meredith rolled her eyes and turned away from the remains of tonight's hastily deboxed pasta, now gumming itself to the plates on the counter.

"Well, really, you'd be doing me a favor. See, I wanted to ask you -- I mean, I know Kenilworth is a safe place, I mean, it's about as safe as it gets, but this murder, it was practically around the corner, and I can't help feeling a little, well, I'd just as soon not be home alone at night, if you know what I mean. So, I'd feel a lot better if you could come too and just fill me in a little, just give me an idea if this was, you know, some husband-wife thing, or whether," she giggled nervously, "I could be next."

An interesting concept, Meredith thought, but no, she didn't wish Shawna any permanent physical damage, just vaporization and reassembly on the handlebars of a Pacific coast motorcycle gang. "I'm sorry, I can't tell you anything relating to the investigation," she replied sharply.

"I know. Sorry. It just gets a little spooky around here, is all, with Alexander working late."

"I'm sure you'll be fine. Is there anyone you could stay with tonight, if you're feeling nervous?" God, Meredith couldn't be expected to take her in, could she?

"Oh, no, I'm okay. Just if I could talk to Alex, I might feel better, and I was having trouble scaring him up at the hospital. He doesn't happen to be with you does he? I mean, he might have dropped by to see to girls."

"No, he's not here. He's probably just too busy to call you back right now." Meredith cleared her throat. This was ridiculous. Now she was supposed to hold Shawna's hand, when many a night Alexander had left Meredith alone so that he could hold Shawna's -- well, never mind. Was it conceivable that Shawna was imagining the situation had reversed itself? Suddenly Meredith felt peppier. "Why don't you pick up the kids around six."

"Okay. Oh, and Meredith, I really do want you to come too. And I promise I won't grill you. It'll be my treat."

"Oh boy. Well, thank you. We'll see."

"Yes, because, I have some news. And I want to tell you myself -- even though" she lowered her voice to a mysterious hush, "Alex disagrees."

"Well. I'm sure the two of you will come to some mutual understanding. In the meantime, would you like to just tell me now, and we can skip the meal?"

"No. I think this is the sort of thing that should be handled in person."

"Well, I'm sure you know best. I'll see how busy I am tomorrow, and thank you for calling. Goodbye."

Meredith hung up. Gads, that girl was irritating. Shawna tried to be nice, or at least Meredith thought she did, Meredith assumed she was too dense to intend the barbs attached to the arrows she flung. But she could envision choking down Thai stir fried bean sprout pizza under only the most select circumstances, certainly not while accompanied by a twit whose gleaming hair and hoisted breasts already made her gorge rise. And she didn't want to give Shawna the satisfaction of commanding Meredith's appearance in order to spring

121

some abhorrent news on her. She was not even going to think about The News, she said to herself. She was a busy working woman, she had much more important things to think about than That.

However, when Meredith went to pick up the kids from their house last week, she had distinctly sensed some dissatisfaction with his wife's behavior emanating from Alex, even his bonding with Meredith against a common embarrassment. If the marital bed were finally wearing thin, Alex might now be experiencing the inner Shawna, so to speak, which Meredith had always suspected was nothing but air. Maybe the two of them were splitting up, Meredith thought, dodging the perkiness in Shawna's voice. Well, maybe she had found someone new, some blonde, pectorally gifted stud-muffin. Meredith would certainly like to hear about that. Besides, on a strictly professional level, Shawna might know some neighborhood gossip about the Healeys that could be helpful to her investigation. And she was hardly discreet. As a prosecutor and public servant, it was undoubtedly Meredith's duty to choke that pizza down tomorrow night.

"Thanks, Mom, you're the best," enthused Lucy, squeezing her waist. "Can we watch T.V.?"

Great, thought Meredith, scraping the plates into a plastic grocery bag, she was the best for permitting their ditsy stepmother to ladle hot fudge down their throats. Well, they certainly weren't consuming any vitamins here, although it made Meredith feel somewhat better to buy, cook, serve, and throw out their daily requirement of vegetables. Sweeping piles of bread crumbs and salad bits from the linoleum under Lucy's chair, Meredith wondered if the child had eaten anything at all. It appeared that, if Meredith formed the mound of dropped food back into dinner shapes with the glop she had just scraped into the garbage, she would have at least as much food as she had served to begin with.

Still, Lucy continued to grow, even sparkle, all to the credit of chocolate ice cream and Trix cereal. The sound of studio laughter floated in from the living room where Maggie and Lucy ground brownie crumbs into the shag carpet and vacated their brains before homework, showers, and bed. Well, it was a nightly ritual, and rituals were good, peaceful and security-making, even if the program was a string of unintelligible sexual innuendos. Well, a little sex never hurt anyone, as Meredith vaguely recalled. Imagine, Shawna thinking Alexander might be here. Smiling, she propped the broom in the corner, lifted the telephone receiver, and punched in Al Reed's phone number.

"Yeah, Meredith? Well, we talked to the neighbors this afternoon. Nobody saw or heard anything last night, you know how it goes in this neighborhood, the houses are so far apart, and hear no evil, see no evil, I don't know. But the interesting thing is, a couple of them did notice a man sitting in the upstairs front window, that would be the master bedroom sitting area, at different times over the past few nights, including last night. They figured it was Mr. Healey, enjoying his master bedroom suite or whatever, although he'd never done it before. Most people pull their blinds, but there he was, night after night, in all his glory. Bob Healey swears it wasn't him, he was in his new apartment."

"So, do you think it was that inflatable doll?"

"Yup. She had it all decked out in her husband's clothes. Apparently the company just sent it last week.

They call it Security Man. You pump it up and dress it, and people think you have a man with you. Suzanna Healey must have been afraid of something, and she got this thing to protect herself. Kind of crazy, but apparently they sell a lot of them."

"Did Bob know anything about it?"

"Nope, she bought it after he left. The way she had it set up, she must have thought somebody outside would look in and see the guy and get scared off."

"Or she didn't want the neighbors to know her husband had left. She doesn't seem to have told anyone, not even her own son."

"Well, it obviously didn't work for protection. The perpetrator just shot the guy too. I don't know. We were figuring Healey did it, just as a working hypothesis. You know, a divorce situation, husband's trying to save .a little money and off's the greedy wife. Maybe he could tell the guy was fake and just shot it out of aggravation."

"Or maybe somebody wanted to kill both of them and thought it was Bob."

"Maybe. But nothing was taken, except the third downstairs gun, probably the murder weapon. We could check for disgruntled business associates."

"Sure. Of course, though I hate to say it, the obvious suspect is their beneficiary."

"Eliminate the stingy parents and enjoy their hard-earned money in Tahiti, at least until it runs out. It did seem a little weird that the kid came all the way back to Chicago and didn't even stay with his parents. Why would he come all the way back and then completely avoid them?"

"I'll talk to Chris tomorrow and see what he says. Though I hate to think of that sweet little boy I remember as a viper in his mother's bosom. Anything else?"

"Nope. That's it for now."

"Well, thanks for the update. Goodnight."

Meredith hung up the phone and slipped across the linoleum to the living room, where her children continued to grin dazedly at the T.V. set. Maggie had coiled into the lounge chair, her chin jutting forward to rest on her hands in rapt amusement, while Lucy sprawled along the length of the couch. They looked lovable and innocent, so easily caught in a web of fantasy. And Meredith worked hard for them, immersed in the minutia of their lives -- was Maggie's gym suit clean, did Lucy like yellow apples or only red, did they know this week's spelling words -- the lives of most mothers, thoroughly entangled with their children. It seemed impossible that a daughter or son so doted upon as hers were, as she knew Chris Healey was also, could pay back this devotion by murdering his mother for money -- and so ironic to imagine the mother lovingly creating the instrument of her own destruction. Yet Meredith could not glibly dismiss it. Sometimes, it happened.

Creakily, Bob hauled his suitcases back up the stairs of his Kenilworth home. He was so tired, it had been an exhausting day, the second most horrible day of his life. And he knew he wouldn't be able to sleep. This was not the fatigue of a hard day's work or of relieved anxiety, but of a crushing emotional strain which would only slowly dissipate. At the top of the stairs he stopped and set down the matching Hartman bags stenciled with his initials, R.A.S., as if he were royalty or the scion of a venerable family. Well, to the limited extent that that was true, that Kenilworth executives were American royalty and that he had created a family tree, it was now in the past. Catie was dead, and Suzanna, and Chris hated him.

To the right, on the ivory wall, cream oasis or some such nonsense of the thirty shades of white which Suzanna had studied before selecting this one, hung a botanical sketch labeled Paeonia Moutan, Shrubby Peony, a lush spring flower which Suzanna had loved, and which he always confused with roses. He had never really looked at the picture before, he had noticed only its general shape and size, filling an empty space. So it was with wives, he thought. They were simply present, aging furniture, comfortable or in need of replacement, but rarely admired or even seen. Now he pondered the peony, its formal beauty, its delicacy and its strength. Suzanna must have selected it from a multitude of flowers, this one had the right colors, it was the appropriate size, or it appealed to her in some inexplicable way. She brought it to a shop where she and the sales clerk puzzled over mats and frames, and then she picked it up and brought it home and pounded the nail herself to hang it on the wall. Suzanna must have performed a million such tasks, and now that she had stopped, he would notice them all.

At the top of the stairs, Bob turned to face the yellow tape draped across the closed bedroom door. She had been murdered in that room, her body torn by a

126

bullet from one of his own guns. He had seen the police cart her away, zipped into a black bag as if she were an unsightly piece of refuse. At least they had trusted him to stay here, to leave that room alone. But he knew the police must suspect him, they always suspected the husband. And he had left Suzanna. The police wouldn't understand how hard he had tried to be considerate of her, to wait until she had established a new life and she didn't need him anymore. He wasn't a monster, he knew he owed her something after all these years. He wouldn't have endured all that patient waiting just to kill her, it didn't make sense. He hoped he wouldn't have to explain it again.

So, where was he to sleep? He dropped his suitcases and walked the few steps to the good hall bathroom, Catie's room once, now covered in marble, with two sinks and a toilet and a tub. Suzanna had cried when they tiled that room, and Chris had refused to wash until he got so grimy that Bob had to lock him in. Suzanna had hung a blue plaid shower curtain to convince Chris this was the boy's bathroom, in spite of their memories of Catie's room, pink and cream and gold, with a flowered canopy and stuffed animals everywhere, on the bed and the radiator and the dresser and the book shelf. Well, Bob remembered too, of course he did, but they had to move on, there was no point in miring themselves in grief and sentimentality. The past was past, and it was better to have a brand new bathroom and a saleable master bedroom suite than a cracked tile bath too small for three people and a haunted bedroom that only made them weep. He supposed part of Suzanna's and Chris's trauma was the guilt they felt.

Of course, he'd been at work when Catie died. He wasn't responsible.

He would have to use this bathroom tonight, since the other one was taped off. Bob stepped in and saw it, on a white wicker shelf mounted on the wall above the toilet -- a fluffy blue bear with multi-colored paws which used to sit on Catie's bed, under the canopy. One of Suzanna's ridiculous shrines, he thought, but he reached out and squeezed the bear gently before stepping back into the hall. He would have to remove it later, of course, he didn't want it staring at him in the mirror while he shaved. He had enough on his mind without that.

Bob went back for the suitcases. He could sleep in Chris's room, the guest room, or downstairs on the couch, he just had to choose. Confronting the yellow tape again and the firmly closed door, he imagined the scene within. There was certainly blood on the rug and the floor. Maybe he should just take a look, sometimes the fantasy was worse than the real thing. But his hand hesitated above the doorknob. He couldn't face it, he didn't want to see.

He thought he had understood Suzanna, but what on earth was she doing with that inflatable man? The police had asked him if he knew anything about it, and of course, he didn't, she must have bought it after he left. Apparently she was frightened of being alone, but the doll hadn't helped, he was just shot as well. Could she have been trying to make him jealous, positioning a man up in the window like that? Bob doubted it, but if she had bought the crazy thing, which she certainly had, anything was possible. He pushed from his mind the picture of his petite wife, quavering and alone, trying to protect herself with a Bob-shaped piece of rubber. But he hadn't abandoned her, she had real protection, he had left her his guns. No one could possibly blame him for what had happened.

Except the police, and Chris. Bob carried his suitcases past Chris's empty bedroom to the guest room. At least there were no memories here. He opened a suitcase and propped it against the wall. He supposed he would stay in here for a bit even after the tape was down, at least until the rug was cleaned and the furniture rearranged.

Poor Chris. He must be devastated, but it was hard to feel sorry for someone who hated him so completely. Bob hoped the funeral would be soon, so that Chris wouldn't miss too much time at Princeton, but the police were notoriously slow. And the Kenilworth police investigated so few murders, they probably hadn't the faintest idea what they were doing. As Bob recollected, there had only been two other homicides in the last fifty years, and neither of those had been solved. One was a woman shot in her bedroom, just like this. The husband was suspected of course, but there was no concrete evidence against him. Well, Kenilworth men were clever, you didn't get to live in a fancy neighborhood by being stupid, timid, or overly concerned with morality.

Bob paused. He thought he heard a noise outside, voices, even a shuffling in the bushes. Maybe some ghouls, kids or nosy neighbors, wanted a look at the house where the lady was killed. Bob went to the window and looked out into the backyard, but he couldn't see anything, only a grassy space and a few shrubs where the family room glow penetrated the darkness. But it was silly to think that someone was out there, that he might be in danger himself.

Chapter Twelve

Wednesday, April 17, 1996

The next morning, Meredith sat on a wooden chair facing Chris Healey, who slumped miserably on his friend James's unmade bed. When Meredith had first arrived, Chris had shoved a heap of blankets underneath it, evidence that he had spent last night, and probably the previous week, sprawled on the floor, while James snoozed in relative luxury on the crunchy mattress above him. Chris's face revealed both his physical and emotional discomfort, his skin, beneath oily blonde hair, a pasty gray, his blue eyes circled and lost. He was, in a way, an orphan now, his mother dead, his father possibly responsible. But even last week, before all of this happened, he had declined the opportunity to sleep in his own bed under his parents' roof in favor of this tight, hard spot.

Meredith had considered asking Chris to meet her at the police station at nine for a formal interview, but she had decided to permit him the psychological comfort of familiar turf. He was, after all, her dead friend's son. That was all she knew for sure.

"So, you're on spring break now?" she asked.

"No. That was last week. I'm supposed to be back at school. I suppose I'll be in big trouble when I get back." He snorted hopelessly.

"But you weren't going to go back until yesterday morning anyway?"

"Um, no. I always do most of my work at the end of the week, so I thought I might as well stick around for a couple of extra days."

"So, why did you come back to Chicago for your break to begin with?"

"Well, my parents -- my father -- wouldn't give me the money to go to Mexico, and I needed a change of scenery. Home seemed like the obvious place."

"But you didn't stay with your parents?"

"Well, I'd thought I might. I got home Saturday night, that's a week ago last Saturday, after driving for fifteen hours straight -- I got home as fast as I could. I guess I'd forgotten how horrible it would be, the rosy glow of memory or something -- I wasn't crazy, but I thought we might be able to tolerate each other for a few days. But that illusion lasted about ten seconds -- Dad and I just fought, as usual. So, James let me pull up a floor, and we really had a pretty good time."

"Did you see either of your parents or talk to them again before yesterday?"

Chris paused. "No. I didn't see the point, and I suppose they didn't either."

"Did they know where you were?"

"No. I guess not. But I'm sure they could have figured it out if they'd wanted to."

"Sounds like you were pretty mad at them."

Chris looked up at Meredith. "Yeah, I was, but mainly at my father. My mother is a nice person, she just can't stand up to him, or she won't." His mouth turned down and trembled.

"So, you didn't know that your father had moved out last Tuesday."

"I wish to God I had, I might have stayed in the house with her." Chris wiped his nose with the back of his hand. "They were still together ten days ago, whatever it was, it seems like a hundred years. I can't stand this, first Catie, now Mom, and I suppose Dad will go to jail. There must be a curse on our house or something, some previous owner who ate his young."

"Why do you think your dad will go to jail?"

"Well, he's the obvious suspect, and he's an enormous jerk, he must have done it, the bastard. The bastard."

He put his head in his hands, and his shoulders started to shake. Meredith waited quietly until he composed himself.

"Chris, I'm sorry to have to ask you this, but it's routine procedure, I'm sure you understand. Where were you on Monday night, starting at about six o'clock?"

"Jeez, Monday night, how can I remember? My head is so fuzzy, I can barely remember my own name."

"Well, you were planning to drive back to Princeton Tuesday morning, yesterday, and that was the night before. Were you packing, saying goodbye to people, having a last party?"

Chris flushed. "Oh, yeah, I remember now. I had dinner with James in the cafeteria, and then he was going to the library. So, I just packed up my stuff and went to bed early."

"You went to bed at eight o'clock?"

133

"Or so." Chris jutted out his chin defiantly. "I was tired, and I wanted to get an early start in the morning."

"And say goodbye to your mother."

"Yes."

"And when did James get home?"

"I'm not sure, I was sleeping, probably around eleven."

"Did anyone see you or talk to you from the time you got back from dinner, what was that, say about seven, until James returned at about eleven?"

"Well, yeah, as a matter of fact. I called my roommates at Princeton to tell them I'd be back Tuesday night. They weren't there, so I left a message. It was around eight, eight-thirty."

"Why'd you do that? I mean, do you guys usually keep tabs on each other?"

"No. It's just that I'd talked to Phillip earlier, and I'd told him I'd be back for some Ivy thing on Tuesday afternoon, and I didn't want him to wait for me."

"So you had planned to leave on Monday, and then you changed your mind? Why?"

"I just did. I was tired, I didn't think it was smart to drive fifteen hours straight when I was practically falling over to begin with, so I decided to get a good night's sleep."

"So you went to bed after the call, at about eight-thirty, instead of driving back to Princeton as you'd originally planned."

"That's right."

"And what happened yesterday morning?"

134

"Well, I put my stuff in the car at around six, trying to get an early start, and I drove over to say goodbye to my mother."

"And your father?"

"If I had to. I went to the back door, figuring she might be in the kitchen, and I saw it was broken open, and I got scared. I went in, calling for my parents, but it was quiet. When I went upstairs, I saw her, right in the doorway at the top. So I ran back down and called 911."

"Did you notice anything else strange?"

"Look, I found my mother lying in a pool of blood. Isn't that enough?"

Chris stood up, and he paced back and forth between the window and the door. Finally, he retracted his fist and threw a punch square into the cinderblock wall. Meredith leaped up.

"Are you all right?"

"What do you care, what do you think, yeah I'm great, never been better," he sobbed. "My mother's dead, and now I'm -- what -- a suspect? But I couldn't stay with them, I hate that house, and my father, he's such a bastard," Chris crumbled to the bed, "and he's going to get away with it, he always does, damn him, damn him."

"Chris, calm down, it's okay." Meredith knelt and tried to put her arms around him, but he pushed her away.

"It's not okay, don't try to pacify me with that stupid crap." He stood, his face sheet-white. "Go now, please. I'm tired. I've had enough for today. If you have any more questions, I want a lawyer. I think I'm entitled to that."

135

"All right, look, get some rest, that's a good idea. I'll be in touch. Is there anyone you can stay with -- a family friend?"

"I'll be fine right here."

"Okay. But I'll be checking back, to make sure. And please, I know you may be anxious about school, but don't leave just yet. Do you want me to give Princeton a call?"

"Sure, that's a great idea, the D.A. calling Princeton. Thanks, but I can take care of myself."

"All right. I'll talk to you soon."

Her forehead wrinkled with concern, Meredith turned and left.

Having decided not to park in the driveway, she opted instead for creating a tight squeeze on the cul de sac. Meredith didn't want to seem proprietarial. After all, her reasons for visiting Craig Snider were fairly slight, some notion of thoroughness and, admittedly, curiosity to see the artist whose wife had recently received a marriage proposal from Bob Healey. But Treena had said that Craig was angry at Bob, and who could blame him? Now Meredith could judge for herself the degree of his anger and his inclination to act on it. Because it was possible, if a bit tenuous, that Treena had lied when she said that Craig was home Monday evening, that instead he had driven to Kenilworth to tell Bob a thing or two, that he had shot the inflatable man believing it to be Bob, and then Suzanna -- why? Because she had witnessed the murder of a rubber toy?

In the heat of the moment? Well, probably some mild-mannered, paint-covered gnome would answer the door and lay her concerns to rest.

The Sniders' aluminum-sided split level, white-shuttered and treeless, was not what Meredith would have predicted for an artist or for Treena. All of the houses on the block looked alike, with a few ranches for variety and an occasional brick front, but basically three neutral shades of metal and a second floor skewed to the right or the left. Meredith could imagine the developer's advertisement, brand new three-bedroom homes in Shady Ridge from $124,995. There were no sidewalks or established trees, only a gutter and the flat, gray grass to trample, with a few jutting sticks for atmosphere. Despite ample driveways, several of the Sniders' neighbors had parked their conversion vans on the grass, as if this were rural Missouri where Meredith grew up, and not a suburb of one of the largest cities in America. Either Treena had a down-home side completely hidden under her Victoria's Secret brassiere, or Bob Healey's offer must have tempted her a little.

Meredith marched up the concrete steps and pressed the front doorbell. A blue glow from within indicated that, unless Craig was working with neon today, he was watching T.V. The bell's flat tones reverberated, footsteps approached, and the door opened half way.

"What do you want?"

A lanky black-haired man with hypnotic blue eyes filled the doorway. A black tee-shirt and jeans accentuated his wiry build, his beautiful head drooping forward on his neck like a rain-tossed flower. Irritated at the disturbance, he did not soften at the sight of her, a mousy older woman in a neat brown suit and comfortable shoes. Although she surely appeared nonthreatening, and perhaps even vaguely pretty in the dim light, Meredith knew she was not the sort of woman to merit even a moment of his time. From the house she could hear the television advertising a brownie mix.

"Hello, Mr. Snider? I'm sorry to disturb you. My name is Meredith Bennett, and I'm from the State's Attorneys office. I spoke with your wife yesterday. She might have mentioned me to you?"

"What do you want? Treena's not here, she's at work."

"Would you mind terribly if I came in for a moment? I'm just trying to fill in some background information on the Healeys' lives -- I'm sure you'll agree that Mrs. Healey's death was a terrible loss. It won't take long."

"You're wasting your time, I don't know them worth a damn."

"Please."

Disgruntled, Craig stepped aside, permitting Meredith to enter a modest living room containing a bleating television on a wooden stand, a plaid couch and chair, and wooden coffee and end tables so battered they must have been deliberately made that way, in an attempt at rustic charm. These furnishings contrasted oddly with the enormous black paintings covering all four walls. In a different corner of each was a yellow vertical slash about six inches long, its significance unclear to Meredith, but which conveyed a vague feeling of menace. Meredith walked to the center of the room and turned slowly.

"Your wife said you were an artist. Is this your work?"

"Yes," he said, his head high, daring her to comment.

"They're quite interesting," she remarked calmly, as she sat, uninvited, on the couch.

With only small louver windows, the dreariness of the April day, and the huge, black paintings, the room was dark, the television providing its weird, flashing illumination. Meredith could detect no paint smell emanating from anywhere, no telltale streaks of black across Craig's hands or forehead. Apparently the muse had departed, and Craig had been sitting alone in the half-light with the Pillsbury Doughboy. He was not self-conscious about his lack of employment, or only defiantly so. Meredith would have snapped off the T.V. the instant the doorbell rang.

"So. Treena told me that Bob Healey made a pass at her, and that she told you about it. What was your reaction?"

"I was thrilled. What do you think? This -- executive," apparently a dirty word, "who thinks he is some great genius because he can make a few bucks pushing papers around his desk comes on to my wife as if I don't exist."

"Did you talk to him about it?"

"Of course not. I dealt with Treena, and it soon became clear that he was not a threat."

"But, Bob Healey could cause a lot of trouble for the two of you. I assume that Treena's work is an important source of income for your family, and that he could fire her for refusing him -- not legally, of course, but it happens."

139

"The man's a toad, and I have every reason to despise him. So what? He's not dead, his wife is, and I didn't know her. I've seen her at a couple of parties, and she looked harmless enough, just the usual boring matron type. I haven't got the faintest clue who would shoot her. Anyway, I don't do guns. If I were going to kill someone, I would find a more exotic method." Craig shrugged and began to pace restlessly.

"Suzanna certainly is the one who is dead." Meredith cleared her throat. "But there is some evidence that Bob may have been the target. It is possible that Suzanna was killed as an after thought. Or perhaps," she blurted, as it suddenly occurred to her, "you felt that if Bob Healey were going to take your wife, you should take his."

Craig stopped still. His colorless face flushed, and for a moment he appeared unsure and discomposed. Then he picked up the remote control and clicked off the television. The room went almost completely black. He moved toward Meredith, stopping only a few inches from her knees.

"Look, I don't know anything about this," he breathed. "I am an artist. I express my passions on canvas." He reddened more deeply and stepped back. Meredith could see his effort at control, his tightly gripped hands and clenched jaw.

"All right," she said. "I just had to clear that up, it's my job, I'm sure you understand. I'm sorry to impose on you, and I'll be out of your way in a moment." Meredith stood up. "Just one more thing, strictly routine. Where were you on Monday night, after about six o'clock?"

"I was where I always am, right here," Craig replied. "Treena comes home around six, and we spend the evening together with the kids. You can ask Treena, she'll tell you. We were all right here."

"All right, thank you for your time, Mr. Snider. I'll contact you again if I have any more questions."

Meredith opened the front door, but Craig suddenly stepped around her and leaned across the opening. "You don't believe me, do you, you stupid bitch."

"Excuse me." She ducked under his arm and hurried down the driveway. He slammed the front door.

What a delightful fellow, Meredith thought, leaping into her car and locking all the doors. He was odd all right, and hostile, and defensive. But she had not one shred of evidence to tie him to Suzanna Healey's murder.

It was about four o'clock in the afternoon, and hardware stores probably closed around five, five-thirty. Chris had to think. He couldn't spend his days lolling around on James' dorm room floor, waiting for sleep to come and take his life away. And sleep wouldn't come any more, only that horrible twilight filled with visions, his mother grabbing herself as blood pumped between her fingers, her eyes terrified with the knowledge that her life was over at its halfway mark, and that a person she had loved and trusted had murdered her. Chris would close his eyes and see bright red soaking into the white rug and blossoming around her like a rose. And then he thought of his sister in her small ivory casket, buried in a hole in the ground. How long did a body last before it disintegrated, before it was nothing but bones? She had probably reached that point by now, just a skeleton in its satin case, the human denial of death cradling the evidence of its finality. His mother would join her child in death, but he couldn't lie to himself, that was joining her in nothing.

Chris knew he couldn't help them now. In his flat practicality, his father was completely accurate. But perhaps there was still something he could do for Dear Old Dad, who after all still walked and talked, living proof of the absence of God, the absence of justice. Bob had moved back home as if he had never left, as if the ghosts of his wife and daughter didn't exist. And they didn't, for him. What were ghosts, after all, but the memories of the living? And Bob had no memories, no guilt, no love. But they existed for Chris, they would always be there in that house. The house was haunted, the physical house, and the House of Healey, but there would be no flying furies to exact retribution in Kenilworth. It was all up to him, he knew that now.

Chris stumbled down the hall to the communal bathroom. He hadn't showered or changed his clothes since early yesterday morning. He splashed cold water on his face, then wiped it on the dank, gray towel nearest the sink. He was in a hurry now, he had to make it to the hardware store before it closed, some store a good distance away, where no one would know him or connect him with what would happen next. He hurried down the concrete stairs and around the block to his red Fiero, its windshield festooned with parking tickets. Impatiently

142

brushing them onto the road, Chris climbed into the driver's seat and veered west.

Meredith turned her Honda east, toward the tollway, and tried to think. Suzanna's body was in the sitting room doorway, on the second floor. She had been shot once in the chest, as had the inflatable man. If Suzanna had been downstairs, say, in the kitchen, and had heard a noise, she might have assumed that Bob or Chris had returned home and gone upstairs to investigate. Her body was facing into the room -- apparently, the intruder had shot her immediately when she entered. Nothing was missing from the house except Bob's gun -- this was not an interrupted robbery, nor was it a sexual assault. And why shoot the inflatable man -- as an after-thought, a joke, a diversion? If both Suzanna and Bob were targets, would someone who had failed to kill Bob still murder Suzanna? He might if she had seen him, planning to go back after Bob again later. If so, Bob was in danger now.

Chris had a financial motive to kill his parents. Craig Snider had reason to eliminate Bob, and if Suzanna had accidentally caught him annihilating her toy, he might have shot her on impulse. As Meredith well knew, Craig Snider harbored no great affection for middle-aged, intruding women. There was also the you-take-my-wife, I-take-yours theory of justice, though Bob didn't seem to want his wife anyway, as Craig well knew. The murderer had broken into the house through the back door, and Craig had no key to the house, he would have to break in. But he did have an alibi -- his wife, who seemed, for inexplicable reasons, to be fond of him, or who certainly might be afraid of him, despite her self-reliant appearance.

And then there was Bob himself. His gun had been used, after all, and Suzanna was a weight around his neck, though she seemed to be letting him go without a fight. Damn it, Meredith needed more information, some concrete evidence. She grabbed her car phone, a reluctant doff of the cap to the modern age and her professional responsibilities, and punched in Detective Reed's number.

"Hi, Al, it's Meredith. I've just left Craig Snider's house. He's a creep, and he probably had it in for Bob Healey, but I don't know about Suzanna. Did you find out anything new today?"

"Well, we did another round of the neighbors, and one guy remembered something. He said he recalled seeing a car parked in the Healeys' driveway around 7:30 or 8:00 the night of the murder. He didn't think much about it because it wasn't a big deal, and he thought it was one of the Healeys' own cars. He thinks it was still there in the morning when he got his paper, a red sports car. Which of course means the kid, Chris Healey."

"Damn. He told me this morning that he didn't go to the house at all on Monday night."

"He did, huh. Well, we'd better bring him in for a statement. We also talked to the cab driver who dropped Mrs. Healey at home on Monday night. He says he let her off around 9:00 p.m. He said she was a normal, pleasant lady, not chatty, but polite."

"Did the cabdriver see the red car?"

144

"He says he didn't notice, he let her off on the front sidewalk."

"Did he see a man sitting in the upstairs window?"

"That he did notice. He figured it was the husband, but he didn't recall any details."

"Suzanna was still in her travelling clothes when she was killed, she hadn't changed into a nightgown or anything."

"Yep. So maybe Chris was in there waiting for her after all, thought he'd collect his inheritance a few years early. Oh, we listened to the Healeys' answering machine tape. There was just a work message from her boss Frank Nelson, saying he hoped she had a good trip, and he wanted to talk to her. We'll have to ask him what that was about. And the ballistics report on the bullets removed from Mrs. Healey and the bedroom wall says that they were both fired from the same antique revolver."

"Bob's missing gun."

"Sure."

"No extraneous hairs, fingerprints, body parts?"

"Nope, but it still could be a careful stranger. The forced entry could mean it wasn't a family member."

"That it?"

"Yeah, just about. We've got to find that gun. We searched Bob Healey's apartment, but no dice."

"Did you search his luggage when he came home?"

"Oh yeah, that was a lot of fun, I guess I forgot to tell you. We asked for his permission, and he gave us a big argument, he's a real hot shot, he's got his rights, you know. But finally he consented. All that stalling didn't make a very good impression, but we didn't find anything, just clothes and toiletries. And a book about old guns, a little bedtime reading, he said."

"What a great guy. Okay. Thanks a lot, Al. Keep me posted."

Meredith hung up. So Chris had lied. He had gone home on the night of the murder, and he had lied about it. Although after seventeen years as a prosecutor, Meredith was used to the idea that witnesses lied, she still naively expected her personal acquaintances to tell her the truth. And while one deception did not necessarily make you a murderer, it was certainly a very bad sign.

Meredith exited at Dempster and headed for home. The police would bring Chris in tomorrow morning. In the meantime, she needed to get home to her own children. Oh, lord. And her dinner with Shawna.

Chapter Thirteen

Same Day

Shawna's glutial muscles tick-tocked up the stairs of the California Pizza Kitchen, grinding Meredith's nose in spandex. Even on Wednesday night it had taken ten minutes of prowling to find a parking space at this, Skokie's latest, greatest attraction, Old Orchard Shopping Center, turn left at the giant metal apple on top of the food court. Although the newly opened Cheesecake Factory had cut into business, the Pizza Kitchen still bustled with late day shoppers and mothers avoiding the purgatory of their own kitchens. Shawna had given her name, "Bennett," to the microphone-hatted hostess -- they were quite the family, these four Bennetts -- and Meredith spent their wait watching Shawna take her blonde ponytail in and out of its scrunchy. Conversation was impossible, what with the muttering hordes and the hostess bleating names, and Maggie and Lucy amused themselves playing imaginary hopscotch and knocking over old ladies. Now they were ascending to pizza land, not a moment too soon and several minutes too late, as far as Meredith was concerned. She needed to mull over this murder case and stood no chance of doing so here. But Shawna had been so insistently cryptic.

"There's just something that I think you should know," Shawna had intoned in her message confirming their dinner date.

So now, because she was curious, polite, and a sucker, Meredith was going to spend her evening eating Korean chicken salad pizza, watching her children and their perky stepmother bond, and waiting for the axe to fall. She knew she shouldn't be so hard on Shawna, who presumably had numerous good qualities which had made Meredith's husband fall in love with her, and only one of which was her butt, but she had had a tough week. They reached the top of the stairs, Meredith puffing slightly, the kids cavorting, and Shawna flipping her tails.

"We have a nice booth for you ladies." The host smiled patronizingly, as if there were something cute about four females venturing out of the house to eat a meal together. "Enjoy your dinner."

Shawna slid in first, and Meredith was next in line. She could either sit next to Shawna, in which case they might accidentally touch, or she could sit across from her, which would force them to look at each other.

"You go ahead kids," she said, figuring correctly that they would fill in the two offending spots. Lucy leaped in beside Shawna and rested her sweet, treacherous head on her stepmother's shoulder. Meredith sat next to Maggie, who remained upright and grinning.

"I like your shirt," Maggie commented winningly, admiring Shawna's vee-necked burgundy velvet tee, a sort of princess-meets-aerobics-instructor look.

148

Meredith waited for Shawna's response, which ought to be, "Then here, you can have it," at which point Meredith could arrest her and this would all be over.

"Thank you," Shawna said politely.

A disturbingly greasy waiter approached and asked them what they would like to drink. Shawna ordered a diet coke, Maggie and Lucy requested real cokes, and Meredith said she would wait to look at the menu first, which earned her a scowl.

"Isn't this place great, Mom," Maggie chimed, pushing her luck, though at least she had remembered who was Mom. Lucy seemed to be in the process of crawling under Shawna's clothes, taking after her father, no doubt, something Meredith did not want to consider even after all these years.

"So, Shawna, you had something to tell us," Meredith prompted, unwilling to spin out this game any longer.

"Yeah. Let's wait until we get our food, so we can celebrate."

Cute. Well, Meredith was stuck here anyway, and she certainly wasn't going to give Shawna the satisfaction of seeing her beg. She decided to pretend a lack of interest.

"So, what did you guys do in school today?"

"Nothing," Maggie and Lucy, well rehearsed, responded in unison.

"Well, I could have told you that," Shawna giggled. "How boring was it, Guys?"

"This boring," they both said, setting their arms far apart and laughing uproariously. This was, apparently, a preadolescent ritual, the boring game, in which they all engaged.

149

"You two are great," Shawna said, and Lucy clutched her fondly.

Meredith had to admit, Shawna had always been good to Maggie and Lucy, and although the rivalry disconcerted her at times, she far preferred it to the wicked stepmother scenario. Shawna was lovable to some, kind to children and wildlife, and generally thoughtful to Meredith -- your basic Disney heroine, including the twelve-inch waist. When, however, the tiara slipped, and she chose to amuse herself at Meredith's expense, as with the wedding album incident a couple of weeks ago, Meredith had lately noticed a change in Prince Charming, from besotted oblivion to embarrassment -- even, dare she think it, repugnance. And when, rarely, she and Alexander were alone together, Meredith could feel something between them again, something more than guilt or unfinished business, a pull which had nothing to do with Shawna. But she hadn't been able to compete with The Little Mermaid before, and she had only gotten older and tougher, like the meat of a retired horse. While Shawna, in the bloom of her late twenties, appeared even more dazzling. If you liked the type, which Alex, in common with every other man in America, apparently did.

Sodas were handed around, and four straws, and a glass of ice water with a lemon for Meredith, to her chastised astonishment. They ordered pizzas with various repulsive toppings, and apropos of nothing Meredith could imagine, the waiter plopped down a plastic plate of cold sourdough bread and butter. As Shawna sipped her diet coke, Meredith suddenly realized that she was very hungry.

Chewing her way through the loaf and half-listening to Lucy's compliments of every item of Shawna's attire and anatomy, Meredith reverted to the question of the big news. In three years, she and Shawna had never eaten together. Meredith knew that she was able to do so now because of the crack which, in spite of her attempts at self-protection, she truly sensed, the weed in the garden of the country-cottage-on-steroids that Shawna and Alexander called home. After three years, the honeymoon might well be over. And if the honeymoon were all there was, as Meredith had always suspected, the possibilities were heart-stopping.

The food came, and it wasn't dreadful. Maggie inhaled pepperonis, and Lucy's cheese kept sliding off the crust and onto the table, causing her audible frustration. While Meredith soothingly carved her slices into neat bites, Shawna set her fork beside her salad, patted her mouth with her napkin, and cleared her throat. Meredith's brown eyes connected with Shawna's blue ones, and she put down her own knife and fork.

"Well, I wanted to tell you -- that is, I have an announcement to make." She stopped and smiled brightly and waited.

"What, what?" Lucy asked cooperatively.

"Well -- can you guess?"

Oh, Lord, Meredith thought. Did she really want Alex back, if he had chosen this over her and cuddled up to it at night for three whole years?

"You're getting a new car," Meredith said, prodding a crust of kung pao pizza.

"No," Shawna chuckled. "Not even close. Maggie, what do you think it is?"

151

Maggie put down her last slice. "I think you're going to have a baby," she said, and miraculously, unbelievably, the eleven-year-old turned bright red and looked guiltily at her mother.

"Well, aren't you the clever one," Shawna said. "Right on the money. You're going to have a new little brother or sister."

Maggie continued to look at her mother. "In a way," she said, "but not really." Watching Maggie, Meredith realized how very much alike she and her daughter looked, the same curly dark hair, the same warm eyes, the same proud, quivering tilt of the chin.

"Well, certainly you will," Shawna said, a bit indignantly. "Right, Lucy?"

"In a way," Lucy said, plucking another pizza bite from her fork with her greasy pink lips.

"Congratulations, Shawna," Meredith said calmly. "And when is the baby due?"

Shawna flushed. "Oh, in about seven months, I guess. I haven't actually been to the doctor yet, I just did a home test, but they're very accurate."

"I'm sure they are. It was -- kind of you to tell us so promptly. I'm sure Alexander must be quite excited." Unconsciously, Meredith pushed her plate away. Her stomach felt as if it were full of boulders.

"Yes, he is. So we'll finally be a real family. You know what a family town Kenilworth is. This has made Alex very happy."

Meredith looked at Shawna, who stared back concertedly, then blushed and looked away.

"Well," Meredith said brightly, "thank you for the meal. I'm sure we'll be seeing you soon, if you're feeling well enough. Come on, Girls."

152

She slid out of the booth, and Maggie followed her. Still chewing, Lucy put down her fork and followed Maggie. It wasn't until they reached the parking lot that Meredith remembered that Shawna had driven them.

"That's all right, we'll call a cab," she said firmly.

As she fumbled for change alone in front of the pay phone, Meredith allowed herself to cry. She had been wrong, dead wrong. She had imagined something that didn't exist, simply because she had wanted it. But now she had to face the truth. Alexander didn't love her, she was just, once again, the punch line to a sick joke. It was the end of everything for her. She knew that she shouldn't allow herself to think that way, but that was how she felt.

"He's gone completely berserk, you've got to help us!"

Bob stood in the doorway of the Kenilworth house in his stocking feet, looking blearily through the gathering dusk at Treena, her hair wild, her hands clutching her children, begging him to let them in. He was so tired. He hadn't been able to sleep last night even in the guest bedroom, and the police had questioned him again today, and Suzanna was dead, and he felt sick. And now there was a crazy woman on his doorstep with her two little girls, and they wanted something from him. He knew this was his darling Treena, the woman he had wanted to marry, and finally, in person, her two little girls. But all he could think about was his real family,

Suzanna and Chris and Catie, and all he could see was a clump of miserable, demanding strangers.

"It's Craig, he's gone nuts, please can we come in, it's cold out here, and my babies --" Treena squeezed her eyes shut, and heavy tears seeped through their lids onto her cheeks.

"Yes, of course."

He must ask them in, they were in distress. Suzanna would have known what to do, she would have arranged cookies and made beds and phoned people. She would have handled the crisis with warm, competent efficiency, for she was, in her own way, a practical person -- a practical person with a heart.

Bob showed them into the elegant living room that Suzanna had loved. They sat on the couch, a bedraggled trio, Treena almost unrecognizable in blue jeans and a sweatshirt, her face washed shiny with soap and tears, her hair looped into a rubber band. She looked very young and shaken, not like a wife at all.

"I'm really sorry to barge in like this, I know you have your own troubles, but you offered, you seemed willing to have us, and I didn't know where else to go." Her daughters huddled against her like snowdrifts, and she put her arms around them. "Apparently that D.A. woman came to see Craig today, and now he thinks he's a suspect in your wife's murder -- I'm sorry, I don't mean to be callous, I'm sure I sound awful -- but it's completely crazy, he didn't even know her. And what's worse is that he's got this fantastic idea that you and I are trying to frame him, that we cooked up some scheme to kill your wife and then implicate him, so that we could be together. I told him he was nuts, that I love him, that I have no interest in leaving him," Treena reddened and gulped, "but he kept grabbing me and pushing me down and smacking me, he was out of control." She started to sob. "I had to get out of there, I had to get the children out, and I didn't know where else to go."

Bob stared at Treena. She didn't want him. She had said so. And he looked at her two frightened girls, and especially at Ellie, the five-year-old, her face pinched and wet and snuggled against her mother's side. It was strange how different she looked now, compared to her photograph. In real life, she didn't look like Catie at all. In fact, except for her blonde hair, she looked a lot like that awful Craig person that Treena was married to.

"I'm sorry you're having all these problems. You certainly can't go back to your husband right now, you need to stay away from him until he cools off. But I don't see how I can let you stay here, it would be the worst possible thing for both of us." Treena's face quivered, and he continued more gently. "First of all, Craig could come and find you here, and you'd be playing right into his fantasy. And you love him, you have a family, you have to work things out if you possibly can. I know what I said to you before, but things have changed. Suzanna and I were married a long time, twenty years, we had two children together, and now she's gone, vanished -- not vanished, killed, like some animal, as if her life were of no significance. But she was a special person, and she was a part of me, a part I took utterly for granted. Why do you only appreciate things when you've lost them for good? Now I miss her." He put his head in his hands.

Treena reached across to touch his knee. "I'm sorry, Bob. I shouldn't have come here. It was selfish and thoughtless. You don't need any extra problems

155

right now. But maybe I can stay for just a few minutes and take care of you a little. Did you have dinner?"

"No -- I don't know -- I'm just a little tired. And hungry, you're right, I haven't eaten. Maybe I'll run out for something in a little while."

"Good, you should, you need to eat, and you need to sleep. The kids and I will just go to a hotel. It'll be an adventure, right, Girls? I'm sure Daddy will feel much better in the morning, in a few days, anyway. Maybe I'll talk to that Meredith Bennett tomorrow, tell her what's happened, and she can reassure him. Maybe he'll miss us. He can be very sweet, you know. Come on, Girls." She took their hands again.

Bob stood and faced her. "Do you need any money, a credit card?"

"No, I'm okay. Maybe a few days off." She smiled slightly.

"That's fine, take as much time as you like. Your job will always be safe while I'm around. I'm sure this will just blow over, Craig will pull himself together, realize what he's got. It's been a terrible week."

"I'm sure you're right." Treena reached over and gave Bob a kiss on the cheek. "Thanks a lot, thanks for being so understanding. I do feel better."

"Good. Take care, Treena."

"I will. See you in a few days. And don't forget to get something to eat."

"Right. Goodnight."

Bob watched Treena and her children get into the car and pull away. Then he shut the door behind them.

From here in the street the house appeared empty. The fake old fashioned street light on the corner, by the curve, cast a glow beneath the bare trees, a sort of Magritte meets the Acme T.N.T. Company. Chris smiled grimly to himself, wondering whether he would ever finish The History of Western Art 101 or, more likely, spend the next twenty years watching Bugs Bunny cartoons in a dingy cell. At least he would never have to see this house again, its prim facade concealing unendurable ghosts. And possibly his real, live father.

But the house was dark, no signs of life. Certainly no Bob stationed in the lit window as on Monday night, the last night Chris was here, the night his mother died. Amendment: the night his father killed his mother, the night Bob picked up one of his fancy toys and blasted her full of holes. So, you see, it really didn't matter whether he was now upstairs tossing on his bed of guilt -- if, that is, Bob could feel guilty about anything. Probably not. Guilt wasn't the sort of emotion he would find productive. What's done is done. No sense fretting about it. Time to move on.

Well, Chris would move on after this. He stepped out of the red Fiero and gazed for the last time at the Healey family manse, thin columns flanking the traditional center entrance, butterscotch shutters suggesting a coziness which existed only in hazy memories. The plastic light on the car ceiling illuminated the red gallon tins he had bought at two different hardware stores in Palatine -- a suburb he had deliberately chosen as the home of the Browns Chicken massacre and several other catastrophes and which he had filled at two different gas stations. Too bad it wasn't

157

a little later in the season, lawn cutting time. Then nobody would notice a guy buying gas cans to fill his mower. Still, the clerks had seemed distracted and unconcerned. And the gas station attendants could barely see him through their bulletproof shields.

Chris pulled the cans from his back seat, set them on the curb, and slammed the door. The noise resonated in the quiet neighborhood, and he half expected eyes to appear in the windows across the street and next door, just above the sill lines and below the blinds. But, although he could feel that thud vibrating his bones, he saw no one, no one had noticed. He tilted his watch toward the street lamp. Ten-ten. The neighbors were all in the back, in their brand new family rooms, hypnotized by the T.V. news, shootings and child abuse and fires only a few miles from here. Maybe they were hoping for more gossip about his mother, how many bullet holes, how much blood, what sordid motive -- they were probably drooling onto their parquet floors. If Mr. and Mrs. J. Q. Wasp looked out their front windows, they might get some real excitement tonight. But they wouldn't. The only thrills they got happened on T.V.

Chris wasn't exactly sure how to proceed, but he could make an educated guess, he didn't go to Princeton for nothing. He untaped the spouts from the sides of the gas cans and unscrewed the caps and replaced them with the spouts. He left the caps on the curb beside the car -- he would pick them up later, he thought, and then he forgot them. His focus was the house now, which portion was most flammable, what would burn the longest before anyone noticed, so that, by the time help came, it would be too late.

158

Of course he knew his target must be the addition, the mammoth home-improvement project upon which his father had insisted after Catie died. Maybe in his own way Bob had tried to blot out the past, but he'd failed. The addition was tacked on to the old house, but it was different and insubstantial, drywall instead of plaster, veneer instead of solid oak. It should go up like kindling.

Chris crossed the street, the gas cans balanced one in each hand. His feet crunched the brown winter grass along the southern edge of the front lawn. He was suddenly aware of his size and his fairness, his blonde hair and pale skin lit like a beacon, "I'm here, look at me, I'm a criminal," his feet pounding in the silent night. Still he continued, head high, shoulders level, he had a right to be here, this was his house too. His eyes skirted the downstairs windows, their dusky black emptiness -- but of course, these were the living room and dining room, the museum portion of the house, where no one ever sat. Then it flashed across his mind unbidden, the thought that had been lurking in the background ever since the initial shock of his mother's death had faded and he had realized about the house and his father's intention to live in it -- that if Bob were here now -- which he wouldn't be if he had any sensitivity, if he were a good and decent person -- and the house, in its own death throes, consumed him, then all that remained would pass to his only son and heir. Continuing down the side yard, he rounded the back corner and saw the light.

It was only a small light, a milk jug lamp his mother had bought and which, to Chris, represented the local notion of interior decoration -- an object from a simpler time and place, completely out of context and electrified, and considerably inflated in price. Through the family room windows he could see the lamp and its glow, for no one had closed the shades. And now he remembered how every night his mother would circle the house, from one window to the next, closing the blinds to keep out the cold and the night. If his father were here, would he have done that himself? Chris didn't know, but he doubted it. Anyway, it was not done now, and the house stood exposed and violable.

Chris set the cans on the grass and removed the rubber stoppers from their spouts. Uncertainly, he began to pour a thin line of gasoline onto the exterior of the house. And then he thought, why hesitate, where was his spirit, and he removed the spouts and tossed them on the lawn and began to heave the cans forward, splashing gasoline against the walls in a robust, passionate gesture. As he splashed he became angrier, at the house, at his father, at his mother and Catie and their haunting ghosts, and he strode along the back of the house, flinging gas, until he came to the back door, where the pane of glass was broken, and someone had nailed a square of plywood over the hole.

Why was the window broken? Had his father murdered his mother and then smashed the glass to cast suspicion on a stranger? Chris paused and pondered, and for a moment he felt the April wind and a chill tendril of doubt. Truly, Chris had never known his father to raise his hand to anyone, not his children or his wife, not even after, in his view, they had allowed his little girl to die. Bob had gone cold. That was terrible, but that was all.

But it didn't take passion to murder, a cold person could do it, and probably better, leaving fewer clues, or only misleading ones like the shattered window. It must be the same old story, some tootsie on the side, and he couldn't bear to divert a dime from his new lifestyle to his wife of twenty-odd years. Chris heaved a heavy splash of gasoline against the wooden back door and the cheap plywood window cover. He remembered the checkerboard curtains his mother had hung on the other side, and he wondered if they were still up. If they were, they would burn like flares.

Chris looked down at the empty gas cans. He didn't know if he should leave them here, so he wouldn't be caught with them, or take them away and get rid of them someplace. He would think about it in a minute. He pulled a carton of wooden matches from his pocket. He had found them in James's dorm room, Szechuan Palace they said, with a flame signifying spicy food. He slid the box open and fumbled with the thin wooden sticks, his chilled hands cloddish. A few spilled on the ground, but he would get them in a minute, in the light of the fire. He struck one match against the flint strip on the side of the box, and it snapped in two, and he threw it on the ground, and now he didn't care anymore. He struck a second match, and it lit, and in the warm blaze of the flame he felt his worries lift and float away. Chris threw the lit match into the puddle beside the back door, and the door went up with a magical flash. He stepped back and watched, transfixed, as the fire traced the wavering gasoline line he had made, until the whole family room addition was encircled in a glittering golden ring.

"Al, sorry to bother you at home, but Mr. Healey's here, and he was wondering if we have a key to his house. He says he went to the White Hen to pick up some food around nine-thirty, and when he got back to the house he was locked out. No, he had his keys, they just wouldn't open the doors, front or back. That's what he says. Okay, Al. Right. I just thought you'd want to know."

The police officer at the front desk of the Kenilworth Police Department hung up the phone and peered at Bob through the protective plexiglass, which he was going to need if he didn't hurry up and let Bob into his house so he could eat a bologna sandwich and go to bed. Bob had taken Treena's advice, which, although well-intended, had caused him nothing but aggravation.

"I just talked to Detective Reed."

"Yes." Bob nodded impatiently.

"He says we don't have the keys, we got in through the broken door at first, and then you showed up and moved back in. He says I ought to go back with you and see what's going on. So, you say your keys don't work."

"That's right, Officer, that's why I'm here. It's late, I'm tired, and I want to go home, and I was hoping you could help me. So, who the hell changed the locks?"

"That's a puzzler, all right. Not too many people here right now, but Ollie can probably cover the desk alone for a few minutes, right, Ollie? Okay then, Mr. Healey, let's go. You got your vehicle here?"

"No, you impounded it, remember? I walked."

"Oh, sorry, we should have that back to you shortly. In the meantime, we'll take mine. You think your wife could have changed the locks on you?"

162

"Possibly. Unless you did."

"No, of course not, we wouldn't do that. She must have been pretty mad at you, huh? But I guess, when a man dumps his wife, she's not going to be too happy. I tell you, women can be a heap of trouble in that situation -- or so I understand. More trouble than they're worth would be my guess."

"Very clever. Just help me get into my house, and we'll call it square."

When Meredith arrived, the air was heavy with smoke. Firemen in thick black suits forced oceans of water onto and into what had once been Suzanna's dream house. Beyond the fire trucks stood an ambulance, its back doors opened wide as if anticipating the ingestion of some delectable treat. Behind it, Al Reed leaned against a police car and mourned the contamination, if not destruction, of his crime scene.

"It looks like they're going to save most of it, just a lot of smoke damage to the main house. The fire was set in the back, that's gutted," he said. "The mercy is that nobody was home at the time. Bob Healey actually showed up at the station, must have been around the time the fire was set. Apparently he had gone out for food, and his wife had changed the locks and locked him out. Otherwise he might have been a Post Toastie."

"No chance he set it himself, is there?"

"Nope. We've got our perpetrator all right. He was just standing in the backyard, watching the fire burn and shaking like a leaf. The gas can caps were beside his car, and he reeks of the stuff. I tried to talk to him, but he insists he wants to talk to you. The paramedics wrapped him up, they're worried about shock. We've got his father a discrete distance away." Al nodded across the street, where Meredith could make out a hunched figure supported by a woman in a white shirt and jacket. "The paramedics want to take them both to the hospital as a precaution, but nobody's budging. Chris is in here."

Meredith peered through the dark windows of the patrol car. A seated form huddled under a stiff wool blanket. She opened the back door, climbed inside, and shut it.

"Chris," she said softly, peering beneath the pronounced cheekbones and whiskers and muscles to find the round, fair face and startled blue eyes of the neighbor child she had known a lifetime ago. "How are you feeling?"

"Great," he said, and a shudder shook him, dislodging the blanket. "Sorry. Don't know why I did that."

"I'm worried about you," Meredith said, bundling the blanket back up around his shoulders. And she realized he had no mother now to do this for him, to tuck him in and stroke the hair from his forehead. "You wanted to talk to me?"

Meredith looked at Chris carefully. If this were her Maggie shivering here, she would say, "Hush, don't talk now. Let's make sure you're healthy, and we'll get you a lawyer, and then, when you're feeling like yourself and the lawyer says it's okay and we know exactly what we're dealing with, then you can talk. You just stay quiet now, and try to relax." But he wasn't' her child.

The baby face of her memory disappeared, and Meredith saw the sharp bones and broad shoulders, the thinned and bloodless features of an adult male who had lied about his activities the night of his mother's murder, and who was found in extremely suspicious circumstances at the scene of what might have been his father's death as well.

"Have the police read you your rights?"

"Yes. I don't care about that."

"You understand that I am not your attorney, I am a prosecutor."

"I'm not brain dead, I understand."

"Then what do you want to tell me?"

"I did it," Chris said. "I set the fire. I was going to run away afterwards, go back to school, whatever, but I didn't realize how attractive it would be. It was like it froze me to the spot. Isn't that funny, the fire froze me, oxymoronic isn't it?" He smirked bitterly. "I guess I didn't expect anyone to notice so fast."

"Did you know whether your father was inside?"

"No. I didn't know."

"But you knew there was a good chance."

"But he wasn't, was he? I can't believe Mom changed the locks. She may have saved him, you know? He killed her, and she saved him."

"She may have saved you too. What about your mother, Chris? We know you lied, that you were here the night she died. What happened, did something go wrong? You saw a man in the window, and you thought they were both here, and you wanted to kill them both but then, when it wasn't your father, you had to come back to try to kill him again. Otherwise he would inherit everything, and that must have been the last thing you wanted."

Chris stared at her. "What do you mean, it wasn't my father?"

"Well," Meredith said, and she bit her lip. So he didn't know about the inflatable man. "You were here Monday night?"

The wheels of a trolley clattered across the asphalt. Chris leaned forward, straining to see the face of the figure tucked tightly and strapped onto the bed whisking past them. He opened the car door and bolted out into the street.

"Stand back, please," the paramedic warned, as he stopped the trolley beside the rear of the ambulance and Meredith raced around to grab Chris's arm. They gazed at the ashen face half hidden behind an oxygen mask. Chris swayed sickeningly.

"This is his son. Is he all right?" Meredith shouted.

"He should be fine, but he's had a shock, a series of shocks, and he won't admit it. Finally, his body did it for him, with the smoke and the dampness. He's fainted, that's all, but I think he should get a good once over. He's a lucky man, no one home and all. It could have been a lot worse."

Chris smirked, and then he started to laugh, hysterically, in shrill, uncontrollable eruptions. "He's lucky, all right. What a hackneyed load of crap." And he sank down in the street and began to cry.

As the paramedics slid his father into the ambulance, Al and Meredith helped Chris onto the parkway. He stood there, Meredith's arm around him, until the ambulance had flashed away, the firemen had rolled up their hoses, and all that remained was the harsh reek of smoke and the blackened face of the Healey house.

"So you went to see your parents Monday night," Meredith said.

"Yes." Chris wiped his nose. "I wanted to say goodbye to my mother before I went back to school Tuesday morning. I didn't want to see my father, I was mad at him -- I was mad at her too, but she was married to the creep, I suppose in her good Republican brain she felt she had to stand by him. I got here around eight, figuring he would still be at work. But no such luck, he was stationed up in the window, I could see him from the street. He must have seen me too, I was parked right out front. At first I didn't know what to do, should I just skip the whole thing, which was bound to be a fiasco with him there, or should I tough it out so that I could at least say goodbye to my mother. I decided to be cool, and I rang the front doorbell, very polite and guest-like. Well, nobody came. I rang again, and I could hear the bell echoing in the house, and still nobody came. So I assumed that my mother wasn't home, and my father had decided not to open the door. I stepped away from the house and looked back up at the window, and he wasn't there, so I thought maybe he was just incredibly slow, and I rang one more time, but he never showed up. Before I got in the car, I looked back at the house, and the jerk was sitting in the window again, as if nothing had happened. So I left. When I came back the next morning for a last ditch effort, that's when I found -- my mother."

"Now, let me get this straight," Meredith said slowly. "You're sure that, at one point, your father left the window, and then he came back?"

167

"Yeah, I'm sure."

"Are you sure it was your father? Could you see his face?"

"So, it wasn't him? You said something before. I don't know, it looked like him, I assumed it was him, who else would it be?"

"And we're supposed to believe all this now, even though you lied before?"

"I know, it was stupid, I'm sorry. I was scared that it would get twisted around against me, Errant Son Goes Berserk, Murders Mother and Fingers Father, something like that. My parents and I didn't exactly have a model relationship."

"Your father says he wasn't here Monday night either."

"You can't believe that guy."

"Looks like it runs in the family."

Chris shivered and pinched his lips together. Al walked up to them.

"Come on, Chris," Al said, "you're coming to the station with me. Thanks a lot for your help, Meredith. You better get back home to your kids. We'll see you in the morning."

"Sure, Al, that's a good idea. We could all use some sleep." Distractedly, she turned towards her car.

Chapter Sixteen

Thursday, April 18, 1996

Frank stood in the shower, the steaming water cleansing him, scalding away his sins. He had no bathtub, just a stall with a chipped tile floor, a vertical slot like an up-ended coffin. But he was alive, and his pain wouldn't stop. Suzanna wasn't even in a coffin, just filed in a refrigerated drawer, her pale face porcelain now, her lips blue with cold, like a bruised doll. He pictured her last moments of life, shocked, then crumpled on the floor, the hole in her body leaking thin red fluid, a river streaming down the floor or soaking the rug or dripping steadily through the ceiling, he couldn't think about it, it was too gruesome. He ground his hands over his eyes, to blind himself to the picture in his mind, and the water washed over his graying head, down his unloved chest and waist, swirling through his toes into the perforated metal drain, like a horror movie that was part memory and part vision, and from which he could never escape.

Finally, he shut off the water and stepped out onto the floor, a clear puddle forming around his feet the way the bright red one had formed around Suzanna. He retrieved his wadded towel from the corner where he had thrown it last night, and he rubbed it over his flabby arms and chicken legs and sparsely furred chest, just as he had day in, day out, every day for years, in the cycle of tedium that was his life. He had enjoyed a few sparks of happiness, or at least of hope, but he had ground them into the dust with the heel of his own shoe. Now the best he could anticipate was boredom, the depressing repetition of mundane events to muffle the ever-present horror of Suzanna's murder.

But it wasn't his fault. He stepped out of the steam into his single room, like a spinster's bedsitter in a sad British novel, a cot and a hot plate and a short stack of quarters to feed the gas meter. Except his room was overheated, a petri dish, the ideal environment for breeding bacteria. Here, on the brown couch, sweating in his undershirt, he had first believed that Suzanna could love him, did love him, that if not for her husband, she would have rushed into his arms. And he hadn't made it up, he wasn't delusional, she had given him signals. What a damn fool he had been.

Frank slipped on his dress shirt, which stuck to the damp spots he had missed on his back. It was Thursday morning, he had to go to work, he had to act like a normal person. He walked to the window and pushed it open to admit great, invigorating gulps of air. Peering out he saw the city, miles of apartment buildings each containing hundreds of boxes like his own, filled with decaying women and misfits and lonely, middle-aged men. On the sidewalk, two old ladies stood in a bus shelter, waiting for their ride to the supermarket for a loaf of thin-sliced white bread and a quart of milk that would last them a week. The best he could hope for was to work in the office day after day for the next twenty years, until he retired and joined the bus queue with a new group of old ladies, his contemporaries, whose husbands were now alive but by then would be dead. And the worst that could happen -- he knew that the odds in its favor were far greater than those for weekday mornings in front of "The Price Is Right" with his third cup of coffee. He could hardly stand the haunting, and he knew he couldn't bear the disgrace.

Frank backed away from the window. He stuck a leg in his pants, and then he couldn't do any more, and he lay down on the rumpled couch that was his bed. Yesterday he had made it to work, and the day before that, but it was getting worse instead of better. Because the truth was, he missed her. He had been so proud, so sure of himself, he had taken control and done the right thing, but he hadn't considered the consequences, the fact that, in delving further into the situation, he might discover, not lies exactly, but deception. Now that it was over, he didn't care what was right or who deserved revenge. He just missed her. He turned on his face and started to cry.

"Do you ever eat these things?" Meredith asked suspiciously as she scraped a wobbly carrot over the kitchen sink.

"Not usually," said Lucy, stirring her Alphabets until the milk became sugary and the cereal was naked and brown.

"You mean, every day I fix you a nice bag of carrot sticks, and then you just throw them away?"

"Basically," said Maggie. "We thought it made you feel better."

"Well, it did, until you told me the truth," Meredith grumbled, dropping the whole mess in the sink and reaching for the dish towel.

"You mean we should have lied?" Maggie asked.

"Well, no, maybe you just shouldn't have told me."

"Well, then, you shouldn't have asked," Lucy responded.

Meredith dropped the two peanut butter sandwiches she had made and the baggies of oreos into pink and blue good-for-the-earth canvas lunch bags. She picked up two rinsed apples and spun around, her eyelids hooded.

"Do you eat your apples?"

"Sure, Mom, of course," Maggie said, and she took a big bite of cereal and grinned.

Sighing, Meredith placed the apples in the bags and folded their velcro tops. "Come on, it's time to go," she said. "Get your shoes on, Lucy."

Lucy slid off her chair and marched dutifully to the back door. Somehow, she was able to put on high-top leather gym shoes without untying them, a trick she had mastered to avoid wasting valuable free time.

"Okay, get your jackets and let's go."

"Do we have to? It's warm out there," Lucy complained, warm being any temperature over forty-five degrees after a Chicago winter.

"No, you don't have to. But you're the one who's going to be cold," Meredith said, repeating her

172

daily springtime incantation, which, like packing carrots, absolved her of being a bad mother while accomplishing nothing at all.

The three of them tumbled out of the house, down the walk, and into the brown Honda pointed toward Skokie Elementary School, where Maggie and Lucy attended the Before School Care Program for an hour before school started. It was seven-fifty, and Meredith wanted to get to the Kenilworth Police Station, where Chris had undoubtedly spent the night. She felt a responsibility to Suzanna to look out for her son now that Suzanna couldn't do it herself.

Because, although Chris had lied about his movements on Monday night, although he had set fire to the house with reckless disregard for his father's safety, Meredith still couldn't believe that Suzanna's little boy was enough of a monster to murder his parents for money. He might be spoiled and insufferable and even on some level criminal, but Meredith could not picture him standing three feet from his sweet, pretty mother in her pink blouse and suit skirt and blowing her away. Which meant that at eight-fifteen Monday night, forty-five minutes before Suzanna came home from the airport, her son was departing her doorstep and two men were in the house -- her estranged husband and the inflatable man.

Frank lay on the bed with his eyes closed. He had kicked off his slacks, there was no way he was going to work now, what the hell difference did it make, what difference did anything make? He couldn't understand

173

how things could have turned out so completely the opposite of what he had intended. He was supposed to be here with Suzanna right now, or maybe not here, this apartment wasn't nice enough, but in a bigger apartment with cream-colored walls and a separate bedroom and a big kitchen they could cook real dinners in, salads and potatoes and steaks. And a real bed, with a mattress and box spring two feet off the floor and firm for her back. He turned over and clutched his pillow to his chest. Instead, he had this sorrow, and uncertainty, and the knowledge he couldn't face.

He had known since last Wednesday that he had to do something, that he had a right and a responsibility. Before last week he had wanted her of course, and he felt that she wanted him too, she responded to him, but her husband was there, he had the superior right. Wednesday morning Suzanna had come to work late, her blonde head bent, as if she had lost her authority, her sense of who she was. Frank had called her into his office, and when she looked up at him he crossed the room and closed the door.

"Suzanna, what happened to you?" he asked, and he took her arm and led her to a chair and knelt beside her.

"What do you mean?" she responded, but her fingers flew to her forehead to touch the purple mass, like a cracked Easter egg, which she had attempted to conceal with a few strands of hair.

"You're hurt," he said. "What happened to you?"

"Oh, it's nothing, really, just silly," she said, and she blushed. "I -- I fell in the kitchen, I slipped and hit my head on the counter. It looks worse than it is."

But her eyes were puffy, ringed with fatigue, marking a night spent frightened and weeping. And Frank knew that the clotted red line on Suzanna's forehead was the spot where Bob's knuckles had broken her face. It was then that he had begun to formulate his plan.

Wednesday through Friday, Suzanna had regular office days, putting her home well before Bob, who had to commute from downtown. Each of those days she looked a little better, less purple and swollen, but her eyes had a skittish, glittering look, and he could tell that she had stopped sleeping, that she was surviving on caffeine and fear. She would be alone with Bob all weekend, and Frank could hardly stand it, but he had to pick his time. On Saturday night he was so edgy, he got in his car and drove to Kenilworth. He parked around the corner, as he usually did when he watched her -- it was nothing psychopathic, he just wanted to be near her -- and he walked to the front of the house.

There he sat in the upstairs window, Bob the bastard, calmly reading his newspaper. Frank crept along the hedge into the backyard. Through the family room window, he could see Suzanna, perched quietly on the couch, the blue television glow flickering across her form like a phantom lover. He thought she was safe, for the moment. Monday night, she would be his.

"Bye, have a good day, Sweetie. See you guys tonight."

Meredith pursed her lips for goodbye kisses, the rite which would permit them to separate from each other in a protective bubble of filial love. Maggie and Lucy slammed the car doors and bounced away, Maggie slouched under the weight of her sixth grade backpack, Lucy still relatively free, toting only her lunch bag and a dog-eared copy of *The Witches*. Off they went into the world to do the work of being children, to become educated and socialized and independent. Still, Meredith felt the silver string from her heart to theirs, always present, but according to her careful calculations, not so tight as to bind or snap. And she felt their energy coursing back down the string to her. They very much wanted their kiss, they loved her.

Greenbay Road featured its perpetual blinking arrow directing everyone to squeeze left, bringing northbound traffic to a jerky crawl. Patience, she thought, aggravating herself would not get her there any sooner. Besides, she could think here, she would simply solve this thing while she was waiting at the interminable red light.

If Chris were telling the truth, Bob was at home shortly before Suzanna's murder. Since Suzanna had changed the locks, he would have had to break in to get inside the house. Which didn't explain why Bob had allowed himself to be locked out last night. Either he had just forgotten about the locks, or he was playing games with the police. Bob, then, had lied when he said that he stayed at his apartment all of Monday night. He had a motive for murder, the classic divorce situation with a woman in the wings and a lot of money at stake. Suzanna must have been playing hardball. And Bob's gun, now missing, was presumably the murder weapon.

Meredith picked up the car phone. "Al? Have you guys searched Bob Healey's apartment, on the chance he stowed the gun there?"

"Sure, I sent a couple men over, but no luck. Obviously, when he moved out he took a suitcase full of stuff with him. We plan to search the house again as soon as the smoke clears. Healey had to leave unexpectedly last night after Chris's little stunt, and if the gun is there, we'll find it."

"How's Chris doing?"

"He's okay, a little shaken up, but he'll recover."

"I'm on my way over to talk to him again, and I thought I'd stop by the hospital to see Bob too. From what Chris says, Bob was home in Kenilworth on Monday night, a fact Bob did not see fit to reveal to us."

"Yeah, well, we talked to Chris a lot last night, as you can imagine. He sure can't stand his dad, though he was definitely feeling remorseful about practically burning him up. But there are two facts I think you should know. Number one, Healey was not a violent guy. He had those guns, and occasionally he'd go out and shoot at a few birds, but that was the extent of it. He didn't beat up his wife, he never even spanked his kids. If he was angry, he'd shut his feelings off, just freeze them out. Maybe that doesn't mean anything, maybe he finally snapped, I don't know. Fact number two is, the kid won't swear that the man he saw in the upstairs window was his father. He figured it was at the time, but it was dark, the room was dim, he was far away, he really didn't get a very good look. His impression was, the guy had gray hair, which I would consider questionable in that light, and he was about Healey's size. But, I figure, it must be him. How many gray-haired middle-aged

guys would want to tromp around in the Healeys'
bedroom popping inflatable men? And then pop off the
wife?"

"I'm turning onto Kenilworth Ave now, Al.
Thanks a lot. See you in a sec."

Chapter Fifteen

Same Day

"Hi, Chris. You're looking better this morning," Meredith lied.

He was sitting on a cot, munching a powdered doughnut. His upper lip was coated with a soft white moustache, like a little boy's, but his eyes looked sunken and bruised. At least he was eating. And although he was nineteen years old, not technically a minor, Al had kindly secured him in the juvenile cell. While hardly the Four Seasons, it did have a waist-high wall in front of the toilet, a reasonable mattress, decent light, and a real door.

"When am I going to get out of here?" Chris asked.

"In part, that depends on your father. Detective Reed tells me that you've become less and less sure that he was the man you saw in the house Monday night."

"That's right. I thought that the guy had to be my father, but I couldn't see his face very well. I didn't mean to mislead you -- and it might have been him, I'm just not sure."

"Could that be guilt doing the talking -- I mean, maybe you want to protect him as some kind of compensation for rather cavalierly burning his house down."

"No," Chris said. "I love my mother, and if my father did this to her, I want him to pay. But I've been thinking, and it all seems a lot less clear. I mean, we're talking about murder here, that's pretty extreme. Maybe we weren't the Brady Bunch, but he didn't hate her, and he wasn't stupid." Chris took the last bite of doughnut and wiped his hands on his jeans. "So, um, what did you mean specifically, about when I get out of here depending on my father?"

"Is that it? You haven't changed your mind at all, you're just playing the angles, and now that you need his help you're willing to brush everything else under the rug?"

"Of course not." Chris attempted to appear insulted. "I've just been mulling it over in here, and I realize that I was being hasty and emotional before. I've formulated a more rational view."

"Which has the benefit of being in line with your current self-interest. You know, you haven't exactly been the model son, you haven't been around much lately. So that, as far as your being a knowledgeable judge of your father's character, I'd say you're not one. You were surprised to hear that your father had walked out."

"I know all that, but I'm giving you my opinion. And I can't swear it was my father I saw in that window. I didn't see his car there either."

"Okay, fine. You're still in deep trouble even with your father's backing, this small matter of setting fire to the house, destroying property, endangering his life and the lives and property of your neighbors. You'll be arraigned this morning. I called a good lawyer for you."

"Do you think I'll have to go to jail?"

"I honestly don't know. You've got a good resume, no previous trouble, extenuating circumstances, no permanent harm done -- there's no gain to society from wrecking your life, and I suspect the prosecutor -- it won't be me -- will go easy on you, especially if your father is forgiving. And there is a fair chance that the judge will be a fellow Princetonian."

"Ah, the advantages of a congenial boys' club," Chris said, assuming a pretentious Anglo accent, "evenings by the fire with a glass of sherry, and Tilly, our favorite hound."

"Her name's Sylvia Grossman, and I think you'd better change your tack from *Brideshead Revisited* to simple remorse if you want to get out of here."

"Sorry. I do. I really do. Um, Ms. Bennett? What about - my mother? I got the feeling that at one point you thought I might be mixed up in that."

"I think you lied, and that was incredibly dumb, but that's all. I can't promise you that the police will take that view, but then, they didn't know how cute you were when you were five."

"Excuse me, Meredith." Al Reed appeared at the door. "We've got a call for Chris, and I think he should take it. It's his father."

Chris and Meredith followed Al out of the cell, down the cement block hallway and into a small office with a metal desk and a blinking telephone.

"Go ahead," Al said. "Line two."

"Hello, Dad? Are you okay?" Chris paused to listen. "I can't believe you're saying this. I'm sorry too.

I'm glad you're all right, I mean it." He paused again. "Yeah, don't worry, I'm okay, Ms. Bennett's getting me a good lawyer, she's actually been a brick, as we say at Ivy over brandy and cigars." He smiled weakly. "One more thing, I hate to ask you this, but I have to know -- okay, okay. Thanks a lot. See you later."

Chris hung up and wiped his nose on his sleeve. He looked Meredith straight in the face. "He didn't do it. He told me he didn't, and I believe him. And he said my lawyer should call him and not to worry about the house. He said the important thing is getting me back to Princeton. And then he stopped and said the strangest thing. He said, ' but only if that's what you want.' And he said he'd see me today, just as soon as he got out of the hospital. It was amazing. That smoke must have gone to his brain or something."

Meredith took his arm. "That's good, Chris, that's very good. Now, let's get you cleaned up for court."

Frank still lay on his bed. The phone rang a couple of times, but he just let it go. Without Suzanna, there was no point. Shutting his eyes, he could see the office, his kingdom. He knew what was happening without being there, it had played out thousands of times in front of him. By now Brenda had tidied up, brewed weak coffee in the plastic coffeemaker, arranged his messages and his calendar, and filled his Boss mug and left it on the corner of his desk. Everyday, Brenda did all that, and it wasn't even part of her job description. She waited until he was comfortably settled – "Is there anything else you need?" she'd always ask-- before she sat at her own desk and turned on the computer. When he thanked her, she shrugged and said she was just trying to get the place off to a good start in the morning.

Brenda had taken such good care of him, and he had blinded himself to what it meant. He had taken advantage. Frank had wanted the princess, not some homely working stiff, the female version of himself. How miserable he must have made her. Suzanna it didn't bear thinking about, it was too late, there was only one thing he could do.

It was calling to him, throbbing under the bed like a telltale heart. "I'll save you, Frank," it sang. "I'm the only one who can help you now." He reached underneath to grab it, but he couldn't quite reach, he would have to fold up the bed first, and he wasn't ready, he was so tired. "I'll help you sleep, Frank" it called. "Don't worry, it's easy. You know how easy it is."

Meredith was back in the car, heading toward Evanston Hospital to talk to Bob Healey. He had spent the night under observation, but he would be discharged this morning, and she wanted to catch him before he left. Just because Chris now believed his father was innocent - - if he did -- after all, he'd been willing to immolate the guy twelve hours ago -- that didn't mean Meredith agreed, especially since their admittedly thin evidence still pointed to Bob. Somebody had deliberately set out to kill this woman, and it was usually the husband or the boyfriend. She knew she was in a rut, but that's who it usually was.

And there wasn't any boyfriend -- or was there? Suzanna certainly wouldn't have told her that day at the Jewel. She was getting divorced, apparently because Bob preferred to take his chances with Treena -- but what if Suzanna had a lover too? She was attractive and well off, it wasn't beyond the pale. According to Chris, the man in the house Monday night resembled Bob, which probably included half the men in Kenilworth and a third of Winnetka. There was no reason to think that, if Suzanna had an admirer, Meredith would have come across him yet. But what if she had? Meredith pulled over, thumbed through her notebook, and punched in the phone number.

"Power Health Corporation. May I help you?"

"Hello, this is Meredith Bennett. Mr. Nelson please."

"I'm sorry, Ms. Bennett, he's not here right now." This was clearly the bee hive.

"Any idea where I can reach him?"

"Well, I'm not sure. He's probably on his way."

"What about your coworker -- I'm sorry, I don't recall her name -- the gray-haired lady. Is she in?"

"Brenda? That's the weirdest part, if you want to know."

She dropped the professionalism and opted for a more confidential tone. "When Frank didn't show up like he always does, and he wouldn't answer his home phone, she flew out of here like a bat out of hell, though why the man can't come in late without her getting her shorts in a twist, I don't know. Oh my God. Suzanna was late too, the morning that she was -- you don't think--?"

"No, I don't," Meredith said firmly, but she started to worry. "Have you got his home address handy?"

"Sure, just a sec. Here it is, 5643 Sheridan Road, apartment 3C. You think something's wrong, don't you?"

"No, not at all, just routine. The best thing you can do for your boss right now is to hold the fort. I'm sure he'll be there shortly. Thanks for your help."

Meredith clicked off, pulled back onto the road, and turned south on Sheridan toward Chicago. In her gut she felt that Bob would keep, but that she had better get to Frank Nelson's apartment fast.

Frank shuddered and sat up in bed. There was something he had to do now, one good thing out of all the bad. He stumbled up and wandered around his room. His eyes rested on the grocery bag that Brenda had brought, it seemed a lifetime ago, folded and then ignored and piled with dirty dishes on the counter. That would do. He lifted the sticky bowls and cups and stacked them in the sink. Although marred with a few damp rings, the bag was salvageable, he could manage with it. He found a Bic pen in the drawer with the telephone book, turned the bag over, and began to write.

"To Brenda Pierce, I leave my company, Power Health Corporation. It's all I can do for you, Brenda, and

185

you deserve it. I'm sorry about Suzanna. I never meant to hurt anyone."

Now lines like, "Don't grieve for me," and "It's better this way," were coming to him, and he was starting to feel ridiculous. He was not such a fool as to believe that anyone would care, not anymore. Years ago he had fooled himself into thinking that Dinah loved him, and somehow, much later and after all that hurt, he had thought that Suzanna might. Well, nobody loved him, and no one ever would, and that being the case, there was honestly no point in pulling on his pants every morning and eating his Cheerios and slogging through traffic to work. And there was certainly no point in seeing Suzanna over and over in his mind, the look of horror on her face, her white body in its small pink suit pumping blood onto the floor. Or the look on his own face after he shot her husband, and all the air rushed out of him like a child's burst balloon.

Frank signed the paper bag and dated it and left it in the kitchen. It probably wasn't legal, but it expressed his wishes, and it was the best he could do. Then he crossed back to his sofa bed, stripped off the sheets and blankets, and mounded them behind him. Lifting the metal foot, he folded the bed and slid it back into its couch shape, where it sank with a familiar crunch. Kneeling, he groped underneath, through the grit and fluff, until his hand closed on cold metal and polished wood.

Someone was ringing his doorbell, pounding on his front door. No one visited him, it must be the police. They must know, somehow they had pieced it together. The noise continued, loud and persistent. He felt the

186

weight of the gun in his hand. The gun would save him now.

"Frank, Frank, are you in there? Open the door! Are you all right, Frank?"

He threw the door open. Brenda stood there, her gray hair and her plain navy coat and her solid shoulders, but her face was white and breathless with fright -- just as Suzanna's had been when she saw him standing there, just inside the doorway, holding the gun. Frank thrust the gun out in front of him, and Brenda screamed, and he pulled the trigger.

Chapter Sixteen

Same Day

Ambulance lights flashed, and paramedics wheeled a white-shrouded form across the sidewalk to the open back door. A lonely form stood watching on the parkway with her hands in her coat pockets. Meredith pulled down a side street, parked in a loading zone, and rushed back.

"Brenda?" Tentatively, Meredith touched her shoulder. "I'm Meredith Bennett. Remember, I came to your office?"

"Yes, of course." Brenda raised her head proudly, but her lips trembled.

"What's happened? Is Mr. Nelson all right?"

"He's shot himself in the stomach. I don't know if he's all right or not." Brenda lowered her head and whimpered.

"I'm so sorry, that's horrible. You were with him?"

"Yes. When he didn't come to work or answer the phone, I got worried. I've known him for a long time, and he just hasn't been himself lately, so I came to check on him. He opened the door, and then he shot

188

himself. It was awful. I don't know what he was thinking."

An officious young man in a navy blue blazer, apparently a police detective, approached them.

"Ms. Pierce, we'd like you to come to the station to give a statement."

"But I want to go with Frank. He doesn't have anyone. I thought there might be room for me in the ambulance."

"I don't think he's going to be receiving visitors for a while. You can catch up with him later, after we talk."

Meredith touched Brenda's arm. "You know, from what you say, they'll probably take him to surgery right away. I'm sure you'll be through and waiting for him by the time he needs you."

She turned to the young man. "Hello, I'm Meredith Bennett, from the State's Attorneys office."

She stuck out her hand, and he shook it. "Paul Regan, Chicago Police."

Meredith glanced at Brenda. "Would you excuse us for a moment?" she asked her, taking Paul's arm and stepping several feet away. "Frank Nelson is connected to a murder we're investigating in Kenilworth. He shot himself?"

"It would appear so. We're getting prints off the gun, and so far the evidence corroborates Ms. Pierce's story. The guy wrote a note leaving his business to her and apologizing for hurting her and somebody named Suzanna."

"Suzanna is the name of our Kenilworth victim. Did he say that he killed her?"

"No, nothing that specific. Here, I wrote it down." He pulled a small notebook from his pocket and flipped it open. 'I'm sorry about Suzanna. I never meant to hurt anyone.'"

"You're right, it's pretty vague, but incriminating. What kind of gun did he use?"

"A weird one, some sort of old revolver, not the run-of-the-mill semi-automatic we usually see in these parts."

Meredith nodded. "I know this might sound a little far-fetched, but is there any chance that Ms. Pierce brought the gun, made him write the note, and shot him herself?"

Paul grinned. "Well, it makes a good story, but I doubt it. There was no sign of a struggle, it looks like his prints all over the gun, and the doorway with the hall door wide open is a funny place to attempt premeditated murder. Besides, she seems to like the guy. Still, I'd sure like his opinion."

"Is he going to make it?"

"Beats me. It would make it easier on the lady if he does." Paul turned to Brenda Pierce. "Okay, Ma'am, let's go. We'll take my car." He smirked and motioned toward a parked patrol car, complete with caged backseat. He held the back door for her. Hesitantly, with a lingering look at the ambulance, she climbed inside.

Meredith stood on the sidewalk watching the car and the ambulance pull away. So, Frank Nelson shot Suzanna Healey. Why on earth had he done it? Unless he confessed, she would never know for sure. And even if he talked, how could she be certain that what he said was the whole truth?

He fought up through the waning anesthesia, the cotton feeling in his head muffling his consciousness, but not his memory. He had shot himself, he knew that, and Brenda had been there, and she had saved him, he was alive. The sheets felt cool under his body, which sank heavily into the mattress. Struggling, he pried open his eyes to see a nurse hovering above him like a hummingbird.

"Are we waking up?" she asked.

"Where am I?"

"Recovery. We'll take you to your room shortly."

Frank closed his eyes. Tentatively, he reached down and felt the large pad taped over the hole he had blown in his stomach. The gauze felt thick and comforting, covering the wound, making it clean and invisible. He was alive, and Brenda had saved him. He closed his eyes. When he opened them again, she was sitting in a plastic chair next to his bed, her hand resting beside his, but not touching it. She sat quietly, waiting.

"Hello," he said, but it came out a moan.

"It's okay, don't talk. The doctor says you're going to be all right. That's wonderful news."

"But I can't -- I have to tell you --."

"Don't tell me," Brenda said. "I know you had your reasons. That's all I want to know."

"But, Suzanna --"

"Stop it, Frank." She stood up, and there was an edge in her voice. "I don't want to hear it. Don't you understand? I believe in you, Frank, you're a good man. I don't want details or explanations. And I wouldn't talk to the police either. If you need to tell somebody, you'd better just tell yourself."

Frank slid his hand several inches along the mattress until his fingers just touched Brenda's. She didn't move, she just let hers rest there, in bare contact, but her lips pinched together, and her chest rose in a sharp intake of breath. He closed his eyes again.

He only wanted to talk to her husband. If he got to Kenilworth around seven-thirty, he should have plenty of time to talk to him before Suzanna came home from Detroit. Then everything would be settled, and Frank could put his arm around her and take her home with him. He parked around the corner and walked to the front of the house. The upstairs window was lit, not brightly, just with a reading lamp, and beside it sat Bob Healey, Suzanna's husband, who didn't love her as he should, but beat her up and kept her prisoner. Bob sat calm and still, examining the newspaper, waiting for her to come home, to his kitchen, to his bed, to his fist. Frank marched to the front door and rang the bell. They would talk, man to man. Frank would demand Suzanna's release, he would make Bob see that it was the best thing for everyone. He sucked in his gut and shifted feet, waiting for this, the most important sales pitch of his life. No one came to the door. Frank rang again, his stomach twisting when he imagined he heard footsteps or saw the blink of a light. Still, no one came. He walked back to the front sidewalk and gazed up, and there sat Bob, still serenely reading, as if no one were waiting for him, as if Frank were nothing at all. Frank rushed back to the front door and pounded on the bell, punching it again and again. He

192

could hear the chime, the melancholy falling ding-dong, resonating inside the house. But Bob wouldn't get off his duff even to yell at Frank and tell him to go away. He ran out to the sidewalk again, and still Bob sat in the window, thumbing his nose at Frank's insistence, as if all of Frank's passions were the merest speck of dust.

Well, he had come here to talk to Bob, to claim Suzanna and pick up a few of her things and get her the hell out of this loony bin, and he was going to do it. Frank ran around to the back door, and he thumped the bell and he beat on the wood, and finally he picked up the garden rake propped against the house and rammed a Colonial window pane until it splintered and fell away. Covering his hand with his jacket sleeve, he reached through the broken glass until he found the bolt and turned it. The door opened, his feet crunching glass. He was in the house.

Now Frank stiffened. He was in Bob's territory now. He had done wrong, he had broken into the house, and now Bob was up there, waiting for him. It was impossible to ignore the constantly ringing bell, the fists against the door, the sound of glass shattering and footsteps in the house, and yet Bob sat there patiently, in control.

Frank could leave. He could run back outside and around the corner and drive away, but then he would be a coward, he would have given up his chance. He had to prove himself the better man, to face Bob and take Suzanna openly. He shut the back door and his eyes raced around the darkness. Then he saw the guns.

There were three of them. They looked like old-fashioned dueling pistols, and that was appropriate, Frank thought. Because he and Bob were going to fight for the fair maiden. Three pistols, but there should be four, they came in pairs. So that was why Bob was so quiet. He had his pistol with him already, calmly leveled at the bedroom door.

Frank picked up a gun and waited, to permit his eyes to grow more accustomed to the dim light. Then he stepped quietly through the kitchen and dining room. Again he paused, listening, but all was silent. He stepped into the front hallway, and finally, poising himself, up the first flight of stairs to the landing. He knew that Bob was in the left front window, the first room at the top of the stairs.

His back to the wall, Frank slid up the last few steps and twirled, the pistol trained ahead of him, and he saw Bob sitting there, and he pulled the trigger once, but he heard two loud pops, and for a moment he wondered if he had been hit. Then he saw Bob shrivel, melted like the Wicked Witch of the West, leaving nothing behind but a heap of clothes and an old newspaper on the chair beside the window. A few moments later, the doorbell rang.

Frank couldn't believe it, not any of it. His first instinct was to hide the body, but there was no body, and he picked up the heap of clothes and rubber and hurled them away in disgust. Suzanna had made a fool of him, she had made him love her and then pretended that her husband was an impediment, when her husband didn't even exist, he was nothing but an inflatable doll. What did she do when she came home at night, his small pink and blonde angel, this paragon he had held so high above himself, did she undress the doll and bring it to bed, did she stroke it and pull it close and do God knew what sick, unspeakable things with it in preference to Frank? The doorbell rang again. Frank wouldn't answer it, they would just go away. Crossing in front of the window, he saw a young man gazing up, and he dropped down into the chair. He sat there, praying the boy would go away so he could think. The

194

bell rang one last time, and then it stopped. He watched the boy leave.

Frank sat in the chair for a long time. He couldn't move, all he could do was turn it over and over in his head, what a fool she had made of him. That's what women did to him, they took his heart in their cold hands, and they kneaded it and stomped on it and impaled it on a stick. And then they laughed. Suzanna and Dinah, how they both had laughed.

He heard the door open and close, and then the little tap-taps of high heels on the oak floor downstairs. He sat in the chair and waited. After a few minutes he heard her again, her footsteps on the stairs, running up to meet her lover so they could laugh together in his face. He wouldn't listen this time, he was a man, not some pathetic, piece of trash, he wouldn't take it again. She walked through the doorway, and he stood up out of the chair, and he aimed the gun and pulled the trigger to make sure she couldn't laugh. He saw the look on her face of fear and incomprehension before she grabbed herself and crumpled to the floor. And he knew then that Suzanna wouldn't have laughed at him, that Suzanna wasn't Dinah, that somehow he had got it all wrong.

Frank's eyes squeezed shut, and a tear slipped down his nose. He felt the touch of a tender but competent hand whisking it away, and his wet eyelids fluttered.

"Frank Nelson, are you awake?"

He opened his eyes. Beside him, Brenda gazed up at the young man in the navy blazer standing in the doorway.

"You are under arrest for the murder of Suzanna Healey. You have the right to remain silent. Do you understand?"

Yes. He understood.

Chapter Seventeen

Saturday, April 20, 1996 and Later

"I'm gonna be a big sister, I'm gonna be a big sister," Lucy sang, her shrill voice biting into Meredith's head like a chain saw.

"Shut up, Lucy," Maggie stage-whispered.

"We don't say shut up," said Meredith. But, shut up, she thought.

It was Saturday morning, and Meredith was driving the kids to their father's house. Although their cherubic voices sometimes pierced through, she was thinking about all that had happened in the Healey case during the last few days. Citing his Fifth Amendment right to conceal the truth in his own self-interest, Frank Nelson had refused to talk further with the police. However, his possession of the murder weapon, the grocery bag note, and his suicide attempt, together convinced Meredith that he would be going to prison for killing Suzanna. Undoubtedly the devoted Brenda would arrive each visitor's day with magazines and homemade soup and cakes with saws in them, and each would derive some modicum of pleasure from the knowledge that he had a special someone, at a comfortable distance, somewhere in the world.

197

After torching the family manse, Chris would miss the rest of spring semester at Princeton, but he would probably return to school after a period of probation, both academic and criminal. This would give him some much-needed time with his father, to restructure their relationship into something resembling a real family -- as opposed to Bob's proposed consortium with Treena Snider, who had returned, for better or worse, to her husband. Meredith clutched the steering wheel and flipped on the radio. She did not want to consider the issue of real first families versus fake second families, and she was certain that it was terribly narrow-minded and impolitic of her to think along those lines. And just plain inaccurate, since second wives had ways of legitimizing their status, even in Meredith's stinging eyes. Shawna had done it alright, she had proved she was not just a midlife fling. She and Alexander were going to have a child.

Meredith reached over and patted Maggie's knee. The new baby would mean a different relationship for Maggie and Shawna, even for Maggie and her father. There would be less time now, Maggie would become less adorable and less interesting. A new family would form, and she would not be a full-fledged member of it. Beyond that, Meredith did not know if Maggie had harbored any hopes that her father and mother would get back together. As Meredith well knew, you could live on dreams for years, as long as no one slammed the window down on your fingers. Now all Meredith could do was peer through the glass, to see Alexander on the other side, one arm around Shawna, the other pushing a stroller, walking away from her for good. The only surprise was that his leaving her hadn't done it, the wedding hadn't done it, nor the fairy tale cottage on steroids, that it had taken her so incredibly long to realize it was over. Somehow she had never fully believed in the permanence of their break-up until last Wednesday night, when she had pulled her fingers back with a painful wince.

Meredith parked the Honda on the street across from Alexander and Shawna's peach stucco home, its crazy cottage roof and tasteful tulip display and neat picket fence. As Maggie and Lucy bounced out, she walked to the rear of the car and unlocked the trunk. The small yellow package gleamed at her, a topaz in the center of the drab gray mat. Meredith looked at it gravely and then reached out, half-expecting it to burn her fingers. But it was just a pretty box with a pearly bow on top. She slammed the trunk and followed the children to the front door. They had already rung. Shawna answered, and they raced around her toward the big screen T.V.

"Hello, Shawna. I wanted to speak to you for a minute, you and Alexander. Is he here?"

"No, I'm afraid not. You know how busy he is," Shawna replied, her eyes riveted to the box.

"Hi, Meredith. Did the kids go in the house already?"

Alexander rounded the corner and crossed the lawn. He carried a garden rake in his cotton-gloved hand. The April breeze had freshened his cheeks, and his still-dark hair was tousled like a boy's. He smiled at her, but his forehead creased, and now Meredith saw the mark of every year he had lived, twenty years longer than Shawna.

199

"Oh, Alex, I didn't know you were here," Shawna said. He looked at her quizzically, his lips pressed together.

"I'm sorry to intrude," Meredith said. "I just wanted to give you this -- it's nothing, really." And everything, she thought, this cost me everything. She thrust the box out between them, but Shawna kept her hands crossed in front of her. Alexander set down the rake, removed his gloves, and took it.

"Well, thanks," said Alexander. "What's the occasion?"

Meredith looked at Shawna. Her eyes were blank. "You'll see."

They walked through the living room, the fancy pink and white interior decorating that no one ever used, back to the family room, where Maggie and Lucy had already ensconced themselves on the couch in front of giant blue cartoon mice.

"Move over, guys," Alex said, almost sitting on them. They giggled and shoved apart. Meredith sat in a neighboring chair, and Shawna stood to the side. "You want to open it?" he asked her.

"No," she said. "You go ahead."

Alexander turned the box over and carefully peeled the scotch tape off the back. He could never rip the paper, he always had to remove it in one unsullied piece and fold it neatly, some economy left over from childhood.

"For God's sake, Alex," Shawna said impatiently, shifting feet. "Let's get this over with."

Meredith looked over at Shawna, who glared at her. And suddenly, Meredith felt her own mood lighten a little. Alexander pulled off the paper, smoothed it, and lifted the lid of the small white box.

They sat there, tiny and perfect, the most beautiful booties that Meredith had ever seen. They were white lace, hand crocheted, with tiny pink rosebuds on the toes, impossibly small and delicate, a symbol of a fresh new life, of love and possibilities. Meredith would never have any more children, and she could hardly bear to buy them, and then she could hardly bear to give them up. Alexander's forehead furrowed, and he grimaced at Meredith.

"I don't get it. Is this some kind of joke?"

"I didn't think so," said Meredith. Shawna turned and rushed from the room.

Maggie glanced over from a Trix commercial. "Shawna told us you were having a baby," she said. "Congratulations."

Alexander looked hard at Meredith. "Well, we're not," he said grimly.

"Are you sure?   Maybe I just spoiled the surprise."

"I am quite sure," he said. "I'd better go talk to her."

"I'm sorry," Meredith said.

"Don't be sorry, for God's sake.   If anyone should be sorry it's me, one hundred percent me."

He stood and left the room.

So, Shawna had lied. Now Alexander would punish her for her deceit, her desperate, silly, cruel attempt to push Meredith back and bind her husband closer.   But Alexander had lied too, he had lied to Meredith for months before he finally left her for Shawna. Had those lies been a one-shot mistake, or the

201

symptom of a permanent character flaw? Meredith didn't know. She picked up the booties and the paper, and she put them in her purse. But in spite of everything, of all she knew about Alexander and Shawna and herself, she felt her heart lift, to the edge of hope, and beyond it.

He would walk from the gatehouse. The day was fine, a bursting Saturday in mid-May, thick with paper tree blossoms and a warm, blowsy breeze, kind and stirring. And he felt clumsy in his car, pulling over to the side of the road and stepping out onto graves. Winding along the gravel paths, his arms full of white roses -- I miss you, in the language of flowers, Suzanna had told him once -- he could feel the atmosphere of the place creep into his chest and expand, so that when he reached them, he felt filled with their absence, but also with their presence, thin as air.

"Hello, Mr. Healey. Good to see you again, Sir. I know you know the way. Just pull up next to my old heap, that's fine."

Bob smiled and nodded to the guard, parked the B.M.W., and stepped out into the place where he could still find Suzanna and Catie. He leaned across the seat to gather his things, the flowers, and a bubble tape for Catie, and a deck of cards, and the latest Margaret Atwood novel for Suzanna. Crossing the park, he felt the sweep of the place, so many beloved dead marked in brass to keep their memories alive, so that their families

202

and friends could find their spots and visit them. For the dead were here, below ground, and above it. Bob turned left at the statue of an angel and walked, more slowly now, toward the beautiful oak that marked the spot where Catie had rested these many years, and where her mother now lay beside her.

Hello, Girls," Bob said, and he placed his gifts next to their markers and removed last week's wilted blooms. Then he sat on the grass, one hand on each grave, as if he were between them on the family room couch, touching their knees. He sat for a while, feeling them with him, and he knew they were there, and he knew also, with the deepest pain, that they were gone. He had loved them both, he would always love them, and no one would ever replace them. He was bound to them for life, and although it hurt him, to the extent he blamed himself for neglecting them, and to the extent to which he missed them, he knew that the pain was good, because it came from love, and from the recognition of their uniqueness. Finally he stood, and he didn't know whether to look at the ground or the tree or the sky.

"I sold the house, Suzanna, what was left of it, and I bought a townhouse in Lincoln Park. The neighborhood's a little young for me, but Chris likes it, and it's close to DePaul. He's decided to live with me and go to school there while he gets his feet back on the ground, while we both do. Can you believe it? It won't be easy, he's selfish like me. But I'll take good care of him for you, Suzanna, I promise." He paused, and a tear slid down his nose. "Forgive me, Suzanna," he whispered. "Please, forgive me."

His arms full of dead flowers, Bob walked slowly back toward the car. At the fork in the path, he turned and looked once again at the tree and the graves, the flowers and the crisp new book and the playthings. He had done something for them. He had remembered them. And, although he knew they couldn't read or smell the flowers or play, his heart rose a little. It was crazy, he knew, but somehow, he was groping his way toward grace.

About the Author

Hope Sheffield grew up in Rochester, New York, and then moved to Memphis, Tennessee, where she graduated from high school. She earned a degree in psychology at Harvard College. Although she greatly enjoyed Harvard Law School, her legal career was brief. She and her husband have four adult daughters and a teenage son. The author now lives with her husband and son on Chicago's North Shore. *Blood Mother* is her first novel. *The Inflatable Man* is her second Meredith Bennett mystery.